The Elem(

Jones, JEEP, Buck & Blue

Complete Edition

ဠ ☯ ಣ

Sandra Miller Linhart

To Maggie
Keep Reading ♡
Sandra

LIONHEART GROUP PUBLISHING
USA ☯ COLORADO
WWW.LIONHEARTBOOKS.COM

The Elementary Adventures of Jones, JEEP, Buck & Blue
~ Complete Edition ~

is dedicated to my own Army brats:
Diana, Tahna, Paige, Marci and Sophè.

ISBN-13: 978-0-9845127-4-4

ISBN-10: 0-9845127-4-8

Printed in the USA

First Edition ~ June 2010

This majority of this book was typeset in Times NR.
The illustrations were done in pencil.

Contents

The Elementary Adventures of Jones, JEEP, Buck & Blue

Complete Edition

Zanna, aka

Jones

book 1

Sandra Miller Linhart

To all children who sometimes need
to believe in something or someone.

Adversity can stress us or bless us,
but diversity will always test us.

☯

"Thank you" to my childhood friends:
Kay, Sheila, Vickie, Deb(s) and Althea,
whose temperaments, characteristics and
personalities all melded together to form a lasting
friendship between Jones and Blue.

A heartfelt "Thank you" to my editor, Saul
Stahlman and the rest of the dedicated and
hardworking staff at Lionheart Group Publishing
who have had unrelenting patience with
and faith in me and my works.

Sandra

Table of Contents

⊰ ☠ ⊱

❧ Chapter One ❧

WELCOME HOME, LTC JONES

"Does it hurt?" I asked when I spied him.

White gauze bound Dad's right arm at the elbow. Below the elbow where the rest of his arm should be was as empty as a tea glass on a hot, summer day.

It looked wrong.

"Where's yer arm?" I asked. Momma placed her hand upon my shoulder.

"Not so much anymore," said Dad, answering my first question. "Oddly enough, I can still feel my arm even though it's gone."

Momma leaned over Dad's wheelchair and gave him a big kiss and hug. When she stood up, I spied tears in her eyes. Dad's eyes were wet, too.

It made me feel all oogy inside.

"Well, let's get going. This wheelchair ain't gonna move itself," Momma said. "Do y'all got any baggage?"

"I have two," Dad said. "They'll be waiting at carousel 3, downstairs."

Momma wheeled Dad toward the elevator. I grabbed his hand and walked beside him. We walked in silence. I had so many things to ask and so many things to tell him, but I didn't know where to start.

Finally, I couldn't help blurting out, "Will them scars on yer face go away?"

Dad's eyes squinted a little, but then he smiled.

"I hope so. That IED did the trick, that's for sure. Why?" Dad wrinkled his nose and made a funny face. "Do I look terrible bad?"

I laughed. "Actually, y'all look a lot better!"

"Hey! Don't tease the invalid," Dad said, smiling. He tried to swat me, but I dodged him.

"Enough, Susanna," Momma whispered. Her face was mad. I took Dad's hand again. I watched the floor tiles pass under our feet. Dad's hand squeezed mine and I looked at him. He smiled, and winked and squeezed my hand again.

Momma pushed the wheelchair faster.

"When do we gots to be at Walter Reed?" Momma asked.

"I report in forty-five days," Dad said.

"Who's Walter Reed?" I asked.

"Walter Reed Medical Center, in Washington D.C. Dad gots to go there to get all better. We'll be there quite a bit," Momma said. "Um-hmmm. Quite a bit."

We'd lived at Fort Benning for less than a year, and I finally fit. I just started sixth grade and Ray Middle School was full of Army brats, like me, so I didn't have to explain myself and my life to everyone. And nobody gawked like a pigeon when they spied a BDU.

"Y'all said we'd be here for at least two years. Y'all promised!" I said.

"Oh, Jones, I know. But it's out of our hands. Now that I've been wounded, I can't rightly stay in the Army. I have to be fitted for a prosthetic arm and taught how to use it. I also have to learn how to walk again," Dad said. "I'll do all that at Walter Reed."

Momma stopped wheeling. We had reached the elevator.

"What about school? What about my friends?" I asked.

"I'm sorry, Zanna. I ain't given it much thought," Momma said in a weird voice. She mashed at the 'down' button. "I've been only thinking and praying about Dad."

She gave me one of *them* looks.

I jumped through the opening elevator door and sat on the floor. I crossed my arms over my knees. My lower lip started trembling. Momma and Dad entered the elevator and didn't even look at me.

"So, Momma, how are you holding up?" Dad asked.

"God will bring us through whatever He sees fit to bring us to," she said. She watched for the number to change above the door, but I spied the tears forming in her upturned eyes.

The elevator moved a bit, then beeped and then the door opened. Momma started pushing. I could tell by the look on her face, no matter what she said she wasn't counting no blessin's.

The elevator beeped again and the door started to close. I jumped to my feet and stuck my hand through the gap. The elevator door opened.

Man, I tell you what. If I were any younger somebody could nab me right out from underneath their noses and they wouldn't even notice. They were waiting at the baggage claim and were clueless they'd left me behind. I was as invisible to them as a flu bug on a crumpled up tissue.

I walked up to Dad just as an old lady put her hand on his shoulder and said something in his ear, then she walked away. A zit-faced boy a bit bigger than me stared at Dad's wrapped arm. I put myself between Dad's arm and the boy's eyes.

"What'd she want?" I asked Dad, pointing at the old lady.

"She wanted to thank me for my service," he said.

"Why? Do y'all know her?"

"No, Jones, I don't. Some people express their gratitude, while others just stare."

"Oh."

* * *

I guess I should really explain why Dad calls me Jones. My real name is Zanna. No, not really. That's what Momma calls me – Zanna, when she ain't mad at me. It's short for Susanna, which is what she calls me if she is.

Susanna Hoffman Jones reporting for duty, Sir.

In the military, everyone refers to every-one else by their last names. So, Dad's always called me Jones... for as long as I can remember. I'm glad I'm his only child. It could get very confusing.

Well, to be totally true, I sometimes wish there were more of us. It's lonely sometimes.

It used to be, anyhow, until I met Blue.

Jessica Leighton Blumenthal, my best friend ever. We met again the first day of sixth grade. I say again because I feel I've known her for just about forever. She looks exactly like me, short and... Well, let's just say we ain't skinny. But, she has red hair. And, her skin is white. And, she has more freckles than a zebra has stripes. But, other than that, we're exactly alike.

She's an African-American, and I'm black, so that's kinda the same thing. She was born in South Africa, like her mom. I was born in Virginia, like my momma.

She's gone to six different schools in six different places, like me. She's the only girl in her family, like me. I'm kinda cheating here, though, because she has a little brother. He still wears diapers. Most boys do.

Her dad is a Light Colonel in the Army

and is overseas, like mine... well, like mine *was*. Now, Dad's back and I guess he ain't gonna be in the Army no more... so, I guess that's the end of Blue and me.

"Why forty-five days?" I asked Momma.

"Because that's what they give us..."

"It's that one, there," Dad said, interrupting Momma and pointing at the dusty, green rucksack just fixin' to go around the bend.

"Could you grab it, please, Jones?"

I pulled it off the track and dragged it back to Dad.

"Got anything else?" I asked, outta breath. The rucksack was as awkward as a whale in a soup bowl.

"Yep, should see my duffle bag..."

Momma hoisted the dirty green duffle bag with the name JONES stenciled on it off the moving track. "Can I put this across yer legs?" she asked Dad.

"Go ahead. I won't feel it. I'm as numb as a frog in a 'frigerator."

The frown came back to Momma's face as she put the duffle bag on Dad's lap. I hung his rucksack on the handle of the wheelchair and we took off toward the parking garage.

Loading Dad into our van took a bit. He could stand but not walk, so Momma had to help him into the front seat. Then, we folded the wheelchair and stuck it on top of Dad's stuff in the back.

I climbed onto the seat behind Dad and watched through the window as we left the Atlanta Airport, and then Atlanta. The trees and bushes whizzed by my window, and silence took over our van like the kudzu outside, smuffocating life.

I thought of Blue again, and how I didn't wanna leave. Maybe I could move in with her. I'd have to get used to her little brother using up all the attention but if it meant staying near Blue, I could handle it.

"Momma?"

"Yes, Zanna?"

"Can't I just move in with Blue?"

"That's enough of that talk, Susanna," Momma said. And that's all she said, so I again took up my window watching until Columbus came into view.

"Dad?"

"Yes, Jones?"

"Are y'all still a Light Colonel?"

"Yes, I suppose I am, but soon no longer active duty."

"What kinda job can y'all get as an un-active Light Colonel?" I asked.

"Oh, I don't know. I'm sure someone could use a one-armed, retired Lieutenant Colonel somewhere in this big world," he said. "At least I hope so."

No one spoke again until we pulled up to the guard post. Momma rolled down her window and handed the guard her military ID card, and then Dad's.

"Welcome back, COL Jones," the guard said. "Y'all have a nice day, now." He handed back the cards and waved us through.

"How'd he know y'all just got back?" I asked.

"They just know," Momma said. "Um-hmmm, they surely do."

When we pulled up to our house, Blue was sitting on our porch steps and she was crying.

* ❧ ☠ ☙ *

❧ Chapter Two ❧

BLUE'S BLUEST DAYS

"I hate me dad!" Blue said, running up to me as soon as I got outta the van.

"Why? What happened?" I asked her.

"Take Jess on inside, Zanna. I got Dad." Momma handed me the house keys. "Go on, now."

We walked hand-in-hand to the door. Blue sobbed the whole way. As soon as I got the door opened, she ran straight to my room. When I caught up with her, I spied a string of snot trailing from her nose, fixin' to smear my favorite pink pillow. I nabbed a dirty shirt from my floor and handed it to her. She wiped her nose across it.

"He's not coming home," she said.

"What d'ya mean, he ain't coming home? He's fixin' to come home next month. What happened? Is he coming home later?" I asked.

"NO! He's never coming home! NEVER! And, I hate him," she screamed, and buried her face in my pillow.

I imagined her snot and tears running all over the pinkness of it. Then, I spied how sad she was. I felt bad for worrying about my pillow, even if it was my favorite.

* * *

That's pretty much all I got outta her. Momma said it was okay for her to spend the night. I held her hand all night while she cried. My pillow was a mess, but she looked worse.

Mrs. B came over the next day. Her face

was as puffy as a marshmallow in hot cocoa. Charley slept in her arms. Momma took a hold of Charley and sent me packing.

Blue was finally asleep in my bed. I didn't wanna wake her.

I sat on the stairs, outta sight, and listened.

"When did it happen?" Momma asked.

"Tuesday, last. You remember? When we got word of the three soldiers that homicide bomber killed? That pregnant lady? One of the three was David. I feel so bad. I was having such a good day that day, remember?"

Momma just listened. So did I.

Mrs. B continued to talk.

"I'd just received a letter from him. He sounded so upbeat and happy. They were doing some wonderful things over there. Building and restoring electricity and water, and he said they'd be home before I knew it. I guess he'll be here earlier than we expected."

I heard Mrs. B blow her nose. "I remember thinking how sorry I felt for the families of those soldiers. I didn't know I was one."

I went to my room and sat down next to Blue.

* * *

I sat next to Blue at his memorial, too. I kept looking at Dad. I didn't know what to say to Blue, so I said nothing. I held her hand and wondered how I would feel if my dad was in a box and her dad was in the wheelchair. I felt guilty I still had my dad.

"I'll share my dad with y'all," I said to her later.

"Gonza, Jones. He wasn't a puppy, you know? You just can't, like, replace a dad."

"I didn't mean..." then I kept quiet for a bit.

"Jones?" she said.

"Yeah?"

"I don't really hate me dad," she said.

"I know," I said, and put my arm around her shoulders.

"Do you think he knows that?" she asked.

"Yeah, Blue, I do."

* * *

"The Blumenthals are fixin' to move," Momma said, Friday after breakfast.

"How long does she have?" Dad asked.

I packed my backpack and pretended not to listen.

"Three weeks, same as us," she said. "Um-hmmm, just three short weeks."

"Where?" He asked.

"She don't know yet. Bless her heart."

"I gotta go, or I'm gonna be late," I said.

"Arm wrestle y'all after school, 'kay Dad?"

"Susanna..." Momma started to scold.

Dad smiled, and tussled my braids.

"You're on," he said, and winked at me.

❧ Chapter Three ❧

THE BONE FIELD

I ran to Blue's house and knocked on their door. Mrs. B answered. She looked less puffy. She even smiled at me.

"Hey, Zanna. How are you this morning?"

"Cool. Blue ready?"

"Hold Charley for a sec, would you? I'll go get her." Mrs. B shouted up the stairs on her way up. "JESS..."

Charley squirmed in my arms and giggled. He put his chubby hands to my face and tried to shove his fist in my mouth.

"Hey, kid, knock it off," I tried to say. But every time my mouth opened, his hand poked in.

"Off. Off," he said, and giggled.

Mrs. B came down and took Charley from me. "She's coming. Her hair isn't cooperating."

I know all about hair not cooperating. Momma sits me down every Sunday after church and braids my hair to keep it tame.

Twenty-four braids on each side, used to be; a different color band on each one. Now it's long enough to keep it in just sixteen, total. Life is good.

"Momma says y'all are moving," I said to Mrs. B.

"Yes, Zanna, we are."

"Do y'all know where yet?"

"I'm thinking Wyoming. Jess has a great-aunt there. She tells me it's a good place to raise children."

"Is that a far piece?" I asked, thinking they might as well be moving back to Africa. I felt my lower lip start to tremble and worked hard at stopping it.

"About 1800 miles, in the Rocky Mountains. You know you can visit whenever you like, Zanna."

Blue barreled down the stairs and nabbed her backpack.

"What in Buddha's name has you in a pinch?" she asked. "At least your hair looks 'tastic."

"Nothin' much," I said, and blinked back the tears. "We'd better get packing. Yer primp-fest made us later than the Homecoming Queen at Prom!"

We headed out the door and down the street when Blue stopped short, ran back to her house, and stuck her head through the doorway.

"What'cha doing, Blue? We're fixin' to be terrible late!" I said.

"Hey, Mum! The wild dogs knocked over the trash again. And, I'm, like, late for school," she yelled.

"Thanks. I'll get it," said Mrs. B. "Run now or you'll be *more* than late."

We ran toward school and got halfway across the field when we both spied something at the same time. The whiteness of it looked outta place in the dry, brown earth.

"What in Buddha's name is that?" Blue asked.

"Looks like a skeleton of a baby," I said.

"No, a baby? No. I don't think so. You think so? A baby?"

We got up-close to the ground and examined the small, white bones. The hands had little, baby fingers.

"Touch it," I said.

"You touch it," she said.

The school bell rang in the distance. We

left the skeleton and ran as fast as hound dogs in a hail storm.

All morning long I thought about them bones. I wondered why we ain't never spied no dead baby in the field before it turned to white bones.

"That's just something y'all don't miss," I said to Blue at lunch.

"Maybe someone put it there, like, after it turned to bones," she said.

"Maybe... but, I ain't thinkin' so. I'm thinkin' we should check it out after school."

I wrapped what was left of my chicken in a napkin, and shoved it into my coat pocket.

"Something smells rottener than a ditched shrimp boat," I said.

* * *

The bones were still there.

"What do you think now?" Blue asked. "Should we, like, notify the MPs or something?"

"Right! And have 'em toss us away like monkeys in a zoo if it is a baby, and laugh at us like donkeys if it ain't? We ain't even sure what it is yet. There'll be plenty time to later on, when we know."

I took the half-eaten chicken from my pocket and unwrapped it. I put it next to the bones, and shoved the napkin back into my pocket.

"Brilliant, Jones!" Blue said, and whacked me on the back. I almost fell over. "We can, like, run our own experiment, and stuff."

"We'll check it every day," I said. "Come on, let's get!" We ran straight to Blue's laptop.

"What're we gonna google?" I asked.

"Baby skeletons," Blue said, and mashed the keys on the keyboard.

"FOSSILIZED BABY SKELETONS FOUND IN SOUTH AFRICA... the remains, thought to be around two million years old...," she read off the screen. "Nope, that's not what we need," she said. "We need pictures, man."

"Try another link," I said. "There... BBC. What does that mean?"

"British Broadcasting something or another."

"Click on it," I said.

"Babies' skeletons have 300 parts, adults' have 206..." Blue read.

"No, ain't no good. We need pictures, man," I said, and walked around to Blue's other side.

"Gonza! Clipart Illustration of a Baby Human Skeleton... Let's try this one."

A bad drawing of a baby skeleton popped up on the screen.

"Well... it's kinda rough, but... print it out and let's try something else," I said.

Blue clicked on the print icon and returned to Google.

"Type 'animal skeletons' in there," I said, and Blue mashed the keys.

"Skeletons and Skulls. Let's see..." Blue clicked on the link. Then, she clicked on 'rabbit'.

"I don't know, Jones. Do the bones look like this?"

"Not really, but print it out anyhow. What else could it be? What lives, or rather, dies in this area?"

"Bat? Mouse? Dog?" Blue said.

"Cat. Squirrel," I added.

We pulled up and printed all the skeletons we could think of and spread them out on her bed.

"It definitely ain't a bat. Them finger-looking things are longer than the noodles in Mamma's chicken soup," I said. "The fingers we spied were tiny... like a baby's."

"Rabbit's out. It has long fingers, too, with, like, claws sticking up at the ends." Blue dropped the rabbit picture onto the floor.

I tossed the bat picture with it.

"The monkey skull has large canine teeth. I don't remember seeing no long, fangy teeth," I said.

"Nope, me neither. But, I don't remember a tail for that matter. Save it. We'll go back and check the bones against these pictures."

She held up the cat, dog, squirrel, and mouse pictures.

"I dunno, Blue. I'm thinkin' it's too big to be a mouse."

"Maybe it's a rat. Do rats and mice have the same bodies?" she asked.

"Don't ask me... ask the computer."

She googled 'rat' and printed out the picture.

"The pubis bone is, like, the same, and so is the skull, pretty much," she said, holding up the pictures side-by-side.

"Yeah. The mouse is smaller... like a baby rat," I said.

"We'll take them both for reference, just in case."

"I'm still thinkin' a mouse is too small, and so's the squirrel..." I sat down on Blue's bed.

"JESS! Could you come down here for a moment?" Mrs. B called from downstairs.

Her voice made me jump and the bed shook a bit.

"Sure, Mum. On me way."

Blue stacked the pictures and handed them to me. "Put these in your tote," she said, and darted out the door.

* * *

I was sticking the papers in my already stuffed backpack when I spied it on her desk.

I picked it up.

Unopened and well worn – it was a letter from Blue's dad.

My heart pounded. Mr. B's handwriting perfectly printed out Jessica's name. I tried reading through the envelope. I spied dried teardrops on it.

Were they Blue's or her dad's, I wondered.

I also wondered what it said.

I wondered when he wrote it.

I wondered if he knew he wasn't coming home.

Ever.

❧ Chapter Four ❧

A GRAVE LETTER

"What are you doing?" Blue nabbed the letter outta my hand. She smoothed it out and put it back on her desk. I hadn't heard her come back in.

"Ain't ya gonna open it?"

"Why should I? He's dead. Anything he had to, like, tell me makes no difference now." Tears filled her eyes.

"Y'all won't know unless ya open it," I said.

"Says you. Just keep your mitts off me things!" Blue turned and walked out the door. "Mum needs me downstairs."

My fingers touched the return address. Some things even best friends can't share.

I nabbed my backpack and followed her down the stairs.

"Gonza, Jones! Why do you have to be so nosy?" Blue held Charley in her arms. Her nose was as red as her hair.

"I'm sorry, Blue. I caught myself lookin'... I didn't expect to see it."

"What did you expect to see?"

"I... um, I don't..." I started to explain. My heart was pounding again.

"You should go now," Blue said, and turned her back to me.

I left Blue's house and started crying.

I shouldn't never have picked up the envelope, I thought. *If only I heard her come back in. Will she ever forgive me? Would I forgive me if I was her? She's right. I'm as nosy as a two-headed elephant. But, so's she. Everybody always says that. 'Here come the*

Nosy Twins.' It's her fault, too. She's the one what left the letter out, practically begging me to pick it up. And, so what if I spied it? Ain't no big deal.

My heart stopped pounding, then fell into my stomach. Blaming Blue didn't make me feel one bit better. And, it was a big deal... to her.

The movers were at my house. They had boxes stacked everywhere.

"What's going on?" I asked Dad.

He sat in his wheelchair, awkwardly marking on the packing list attached to the clipboard, which rested on his lap.

He stayed at home all the time now because there were no ramps for his chair. The housing office didn't think it was necessary to put any up, since we were fixin' to leave and all.

"Movers. You'd think you'd know this part by now," Dad said with a wink, and then he frowned. "Hey, Jones, you look like you've been crying. Everything okay?"

I shrugged. "Why'd they come so soon? We got three weeks yet, don't we?"

"We're putting most of it in storage. We'll be at Walter Reed for a bit. And, we can't live here any longer. They need the house for another family ASAP," Dad said. "Hey, is that why you're upset? Because we're leaving?"

"Oh, Daddy, I did something terrible bad and now Blue hates me!"

I put my head on his armrest and cried.

"Hey. Hey, now." Dad's hand rubbed my back. "What happened?"

I told him about the letter and Blue walking in on me and how she'd never wanna see me again.

Dad smiled. "Jones, it's not you. Blue's having a hard time. She'll talk to you when she's ready."

"So, y'all don't think she hates me?"

"No, Jones, I don't," he said. "What do you think you can do to let her know you're sorry?"

"I dunno," I said. "What?"

"You need to figure that one out for yourself, my girl. So, while you're thinking on it, I need you to go upstairs and put the clothes you don't want packed in the corner of your room, along with anything you can't live without for about six months. Okay?"

"'Kay. Thanks, Dad," I said, and gave him a big hug. "Where's Momma got off to?"

"She had to run some errands. She'll be back with Hawaiian Pizza directly. Can't beat that with a dead skunk. Now, go," Dad said.

* * *

"Where we fixin' to stay tonight?" I asked.

Boxes were piled to the ceiling in some places. The movers had wrapped our furniture and beds in plastic and lined them up against the wall. They were fixin' to come back in the morning to load the truck and take it all away.

"Base lodging has room for us for about two weeks while I out-process and get all the paperwork ready for our trip," Dad said, taking a big bite of pizza.

"How far away is base lodging?"

"Just yonder, across that field there. Don't worry, Jones. Blue is still within walking distance... well, for you anyway." Dad smiled.

"With the Good Lord's help, y'all be walking again soon, Reg," Momma said.

Momma got more positive about Dad since Mr. B's memorial. I think she spied what could've been and started counting them blessings of hers again.

"And, I'll not be more than an arm's length away..." She said.

"Is that one of your arms, or mine?" Dad asked.

"Funny, Mister." Momma sat in Dad's lap and kissed him.

"Eww... give a girl a break, would ya? Is this the way y'all act around a kid?" I pretended to gag.

"Bless yer heart, child. Why don'cha go down to Jess' and see if she wants to stay at the motel with you tonight. Y'all got yer own room," said Momma. "And, there's a hot tub, to boot."

I looked at Dad. He shrugged.

"Did I miss something?" asked Momma.

"No. Not really." I nabbed my coat and headed out the door to see if Blue wanted to sleep over with me.

I didn't think she would.

* * *

"She's upstairs. Go on up," Mrs. B said. Charley sat in his highchair, throwing peas.

Blue was sitting on her bed. I watched her turn the letter over in her hands.

She looked up.

"He sent it, like, the day before," she said, pointing at the postmark.

"Yeah?" I couldn't think of anything else to say.

I sat down beside her on her bed.

"It feels as if he had a lot to say." She weighed it in her hand.

"It does look like a lot of paper."

"Will you read it?" she asked. "I mean, would you read it first and let me know what it says?"

"Um, sure... yeah... I guess. If y'all want me to."

She didn't hand it to me. I didn't try to take it.

We sat for a bit.

She looked at me as if she noticed me for the first time.

"Why are you here?" she asked.

"I, uh... D'ya wanna sleep over with me in the base lodging motel place yonder? I got my own room, and..."

"Could be 'tastic," she said, but her voice was as flat as a well-worn tire, and she looked like a zombie from the movies. "I'll go ask me mum."

* * *

"Dad, can we walk to the motel?" Blue and I had our backpacks and flashlights. Our suitcases were packed in the van.

"Help Momma get me out of the house and into the van. Then you can go," Dad said.

It was way easier with Blue's help. The stairs were a buzzard, though, and twice we almost dumped Dad.

"Oh, Bless the Lord, that's a job. Um-hmmm, quite a job," Momma said. "Say good-bye to this old house, y'all. We won't be coming back."

It's always hard to say good-bye to a place of yer life. This time wasn't no easier.

I took Blue's hand and knew she'd be leaving soon, too. I wanted to cry. My dad-burned lip started to tremble. Again. Man, I was fixin' to turn into a real baby, like Charley.

"Y'all be careful in the field. Hear me? Very careful. Do y'all got that cell phone of yours, Jess?" Momma asked.

"Yes, Mrs. J."

"Alrighty, then," said Dad. "Don't take too long. You know how your Momma worries."

* * *

Blue and I headed across the field.

"You still have the printouts?" she asked.

"Yep. Think we'll be able to spy it in the dark?"

"Who knows?"

We didn't need to worry. The whiteness of the bones glowed in the beam of the flashlight. I sat down next to them and started digging in my backpack.

"Gonza, Jones! Watch it! You're, like, sitting on a big pile of ants!"

I jumped up in the nick of time and knocked the fire ants from my shoes.

They're nasty little buggers. They hurt terrible bad when they bite. And, man, they bite like a starving mutt at an outdoor barbeque.

Blue held her light's beam on me so I could get 'em all off. Then, I pulled a magnifying glass from my bag and shined the light on the bones.

"Look at that, would'ya?" I said.

The chicken bones lay as bare as the other ones, only not as white.

"The ants totally stripped the chicken down to the bare nubbins." I poked at the bones with a stick.

"The sun must, like, bleach them."

"Well, now we know why we ain't spied them before. They ain't been here that long."

CRASH!

The loudness made us both jump.

"Aaahhh!" one of us screamed.

Maybe both of us.

We turned our flashlights to the sound and wrapped our arms around each other.

"What was that?" I asked. I felt Blue shaking. Or maybe it was me.

Our lights searched the night.

I heard a sound like a glass bottle rolling on the pavement.

Our beams caught on a tipped garbage can.

"Bloody dogs! They did it again," Blue said, and relaxed her grip on me.

A flash of fur popped outta the can like a jack-in-the-box, and two red eyes peered at us.

"I'm thinkin' it ain't no dog," I said. "Very slowly... pick up yer backpack..."

I lifted mine.

"Got it?" I asked.

"Yes..." she whispered.

Our lights held on to the glowing red eyes. They seemed to be coming closer.

"RUN!" We both yelled together, and took off.

I looked behind me.

I could see nothing in the night, but I thought I heard something coming closer.

"Run faster!" I screamed. "It's coming."

~ Chapter Five ~

HOME AWAY FROM HOME

"Just in time," Momma said, as Blue and I ran outta the field and into the motel parking lot. "Get Dad's chair from the back, would y'all? Lordy! Y'all are breathing hard."

"Ran... Had to... Big monster... Red eyes..." Blue said, between gulps of air.

"Bless yer little hearts. Y'all are too silly!" Momma said, shaking her head. She handed the van keys to me. "Um-hmmm, too, too silly."

"No, really..." I tried to explain.

"Later. Just be gettin' that chair, Zanna. Let's get unpacked, and then y'all can tell us all about yer little monster."

"Big monster," I mumbled.

Blue and I wrestled the chair outta the back. We helped Momma help Dad into it. She gave us our room key card.

"32 – there," she said, pointing. "We're right next door – room 30. Now, y'all go get ready for bed. And, don't forget them bags."

"Dad, don't forget yer bag," I said, pointing at Momma.

Dad laughed.

"Y'all better run, child," Momma said.

Blue and I nabbed our bags and ran to our door, giggling.

* * *

We sat on the big bed in our pajamas. Pictures of bones lay all around us.

"I wish we had, like, more time to look at it," Blue said.

"Yeah, me too."

"I think the rat and squirrel are definitely out."

"Yeah, me too," I said.

"I'm hungry."

"Yeah, me too."

"Gonza, Jones. Is that all you can say?"

"Nope."

"What do you think it was?"

"The monster? I ain't thinkin' it's a dog," I said.

"Me neither."

The knock on the door startled us both.

Blue went to the door and tiptoed to look out through the peephole.

"Who is it?" Blue called through the door.

"It's Momma, Zanna. Open the door, please."

"How do we know it's Momma?" I asked.

"Because I said so," said Momma.

"Y'all always lie," I said.

"OPEN THE DOOR!"

Blue opened the door and Momma came rushing in. She grabbed me and threw me down on the bed and tickled me.

"Lie, do I? I'll show y'all a lie."

"Stop! Stop! Uncle! I call uncle," I screamed with laughter.

"Ya better call aunt!" Momma said, and stopped tickling me. "Do y'all got everything ya need?"

"We're hungry."

"Yes, we're hungry," Blue echoed.

Momma reached into her pocket and pulled out four, one dollar bills.

"This should be enough for y'all to get a cold drink and a snack. I'll wait here until y'all get back," she said, and then added, "Lordy, child, I can't believe y'all are hungry after three large slices of pizza! Bless yer heart."

Blue and I ran barefoot in our pajamas to the vending machines outside the motel.

"What would you like? Cola or Dr. Pibb?" Blue asked.

"Dr. Pibb. What d'ya want? Cheese puffs or corn chips?"

"Corn chips," Blue said.

"D'ya smell that?" I asked, sniffing the air as I mashed the button for corn chips.

The machine made a loud, whirring noise, and mashed the chips to the glass. They dropped to the bottom with a thud. A Dr. Pibb fell in Blue's machine.

A rapid, chattering sound came from around the corner.

"Gonza, Jones! What was that?" Blue asked, holding her breath. "Should we check it out?"

The chatter came again. The hair on the back of my neck rose like a choir group in church.

"I ain't thinkin' so," I said. "Let's just get our stuff and go."

I mashed the button for cheese puffs. The whirring sound, then the thud, then another loud chatter from around the corner. I reached in and nabbed both bags. My eyes didn't leave the corner where the chatter sound came.

"Blue, d'ya hear me?"

Blue edged her way to the corner... toward the chatter-chitter sound. Papers rustled and a screechy chatter followed. Blue froze.

"Blue!" I moved closer to her. "Blue! Come back!"

She took another step.

The chatter became a shrill chirping. I noticed the smell of rotting food again and spied the edge of a dumpster peeking around the corner.

"Something is in the trash," she said.

"No? Really? I never woulda guessed."

Blue smirked at me. "Go see what it is."

"You go see what it is."

"Okay."

"No! Wait! Blue! Let's check it out tomorrow. When it's light out. Come on. Momma's waiting for us. She's gonna be madder than a bull in the milking line."

My heart raced. I prayed she'd listen to me.

She turned around and walked back to the vending machines.

"Okay. We'll check it out tomorrow... you big pansy," she said as she passed me.

But I could tell she was relieved, too.

She nabbed the Pibb and put the other dollar into the machine. She mashed the Cola button. The loud, clunking noise deposited another cold drink and made whatever was in the dumpster screech again. Blue nabbed her drink and we ran back to our room.

"You don't think it was, like, the monster from me trash, do you?" Blue asked between gulps of Cola.

"Everything's possible."

"Should we have maybe told your mom?"

"Heck, no. She'd never let us get stuff by ourselves again. Or worse, she'd make fun of our 'little' monster, bless our hearts." I said, through bites of cheese puffs. I felt safe in our room with the door bolted and locked. Whatever had chattered at us outside would stay outside.

* * *

I woke up when the sun lit up the curtains like fire in our room. I spied the clock.

According to the flashing display, it was 6:32.

"Blue? Y'all awake?"

"Nope."

"Get up. We got a dumpster to check out," I said in her face. Then, I jumped outta bed and started pulling on my pants.

"Gonza, Jones! Brush your teeth. Your breath is bloody nasty." Blue pulled the covers up over her face. "What time is it, anyway?"

"8:30," I lied. I ran to the bathroom and brushed my teeth.

* * *

"Come on!" I said, holding the door open.

"Hold on! For Buddha's sake, let me get me shoes tied."

She was finally dressed and ready, thanks to my prodding.

"Okay. Let's go. What's holding you?" she asked, and ran out.

The stink by the dumpster made me gag. I spied Blue pinching her nose closed.

"Does that help?" I asked.

"Duddent hirt," she said through plugged nostrils.

I clamped my nose shut. "D'ya thee anythink?"

"Doe. Wait. There are thum, like, hand printh in thith ithe queem," she said.

"Ithe queem? What the heck ith ithe queem?" I looked to where she pointed and spied some melted, dried ice cream on the ground. In it were bitty little prints, just like the hands of the skeleton we were investigating. I unplugged my nose.

"Is it the ghost of our baby in the field?" I asked.

"Could be," she said, her nose still plugged.

"Do ghosts leave hand printh?"

A loud, rustling noise came from the dumpster, making us both jump.

We ran back to our room and I grabbed the knob.

It was locked.

Our door was locked.

Our door was locked and there was probably most likely something after us.

I ran to room 30 and knocked on the door.

"What? Who is it?" Momma called through the door.

"Momma, it's me. We locked ourselves out. Momma! Quick! Let us in."

I knocked harder and faster. I heard the ghost baby coming around the corner.

I heard it breathing.

It was gonna start crying at any second.

"Momma!"

"Goodness, child. Hold yer horses,"

Momma said, opening the door. "What has yer braids in a knot?"

"Something's behind me," I said, and ran into her room. Blue followed.

"What in heaven's name is behind y'all, besides Jess?" Momma asked, sticking her head out the door. "My goodness, child, what are y'all doing up at a ten to seven on this Blessed Saturday morning? Haven't y'all ever heard of sleeping in?"

"Ten to seven!?" Blue asked in disbelief. She threw a pillow at me.

She missed everything but my face.

* *

❧ Chapter Six ❧

GHOST BABY'S BONES

"Dad?"

"Yes, Jones?"

"Where is the rest of yer arm?" I asked.

We were at Burger King finishing breakfast. Blue's mom had called her and needed help with Charley while the movers packed their house. Blue was fixin' to meet me back at the motel in about two hours.

"Well... when the bomb exploded, it took most of my arm with it," said Dad.

"Nothin' left?" I asked.

"Bits and pieces, I guess. I wasn't in any position to notice."

"So, parts of yer arm could be lying in the desert somewhere?" I asked. "Waiting for some kid to find 'em in some yonder field like eggs at an Easter hunt?"

I thought about our baby skeleton and shivered.

"No. Not like that. The medics pick up the parts they find and evacuate them with the injured. They try to reattach what they can, and incinerate parts they can't identify. They try to keep your parts with you. They do the best they can," he said.

"So they ain't never found no more of yer arm?" I popped another bit of hash browns into my mouth.

"They found my finger, I'm told."

"Which one?"

"Does it matter?"

"I guess not," I said. "What happened to it?"

"I signed a form saying they could dispose of it."

"Why would'ya have to do that?"

"Some soldiers' religions state they have to be buried with all their parts."

"Why didn't y'all keep the finger?" I asked.

"Why should I?"

"I dunno. Y'all could use it as a pointer, or frame it, or something," I said.

"Heaven help us, Zanna. Bless yer heart. Y'all are one strange girl," Momma said. "Are y'all finished?"

I didn't know if she meant with breakfast, or my questions. So, I nodded, and started clearing the table.

* * *

"Do you have them," Blue asked.

"Yeah." I pulled the folded sheets of paper from my back pocket. They were all scrunched.

The bones glared at us from the field. We finally had more time to examine them, and it wasn't dark out. Bonus!

"The hand is definitely a baby's," Blue said.

"But the skull ain't." I pointed out the way the face sloped a little where the eye sockets were. It looked like a small snout.

"Gonza! Maybe that's how the baby died. Maybe it was, like, deformed, or stillborn."

"Maybe. But who'd leave a baby in a field? Dead or alive?"

"I heard the other day that Hannah – that tall girl in 8th grade? You know, the one who's always so snotty and bossy to us?" Her eyes were wide.

I nodded. I knew who she meant.

Blue continued. "Well, anyway, I heard she was pregnant a while ago and then she wasn't."

"What d'ya mean, she was pregnant, then wasn't? She's right near our age. How could she be pregnant?"

Blue raised her left eyebrow at me.

I like it when she does that. I've tried a bunch of times, but just succeed in raising both eyebrows and look surprised.

"Jones..."

"I know, I know. But, how d'ya be pregnant one minute and not the next?"

"That's what I'm saying... Maybe Hannah came out here one night and, like, left her baby here."

"I think yer as cracked as a year old walnut."

"I might be, but that doesn't make me wrong," she said.

"Don't make ya right, neither."

The thought of someone leaving a baby, dead or alive in the field made me sadder than a French Poodle in tights.

It didn't feel like a very Christian thing to do.

"Bless its heart. I'm thinkin' we should bury the poor thing," I said. "I mean, after we're done investigating it and all."

"That's a brilliant idea, Jones."

I spread the pictures out around the bones, carefully avoiding the ant pile.

The back of the skeleton had been partially buried by the wind, but most of the pelvic bone was showing.

"Look. See how the pubis on the rat is flatter than a doorstop?" I asked.

"Yes. Mouse and rat are both out, just as we thought."

Blue tore the pages in two and shoved them into her back pocket.

"Squirrel's too small," she added, and tore that page, too.

"Baby, monkey, dog, cat... Gonza, Jones, I don't think it looks much like any of these. The skull, like..."

A loud crash came from the same trash cans the monster was in last night.

We jumped up faster than lightning in a hot tub.

I spied a ringed tail go 'round the side of the garage.

"What was that?" I asked.

Blue's phone jingled a tune I couldn't put my finger on, but I knew I knew it. It was the Beatles, or something. Knowing Blue, it was the Beatles. She loved the Beatles.

"Hello?" Blue answered the phone. "Yes, Mum. No, we aren't busy... Sure thing.

Right there... Bye."

The one-sided conversation told me we were fixin' to leave the ghost baby's bones for later.

☙ Chapter Seven ❧

CHANGE OF PLANS

"We've been doing some talking and we've come to a decision we think y'all will cotton to.

"Now, I know, Zanna, it might be hard at first, but we need to know y'all give it a try," Momma said.

Charley played on the floor in Blue's living room, surrounded by packing paper.

Momma sat to the right of me on the couch. Dad was seated to my left in his chair.

Mrs. B sat in the recliner; Blue on the armrest.

"It will take some adjustments on all our parts, but I think it may be a fun adventure," Mrs. B said.

"What?" Blue asked.

"Now, before you get too excited, or too upset, hear us out," Dad said.

"What?" I asked.

The suspense was too much.

"Well..." Momma started.

"We've been talking," Dad said.

"We think it may be a good idea... well, in fact, the best thing for everyone..." Mrs. B said.

"WHAT!?" Blue and I asked together.

Charley looked up from the floor. His lower lip trembled.

Mrs. B reached out and tossed him a toy. He giggled, and then went back to playing with the paper.

"For goodness sake, girls! Be patient," Mrs. B said.

"Sorry," Blue said.

"It's just that y'all are taking forever," I said.

"Bless yer hearts," Momma said.

"Now, y'all don't say nothin' until we're done talkin'. Then y'all can ask questions. Okay? Any questions at all," she added.

"Deal," I said, and sighed heavier than a sliced blimp.

"We've been discussing the possibility of y'all moving to Wyoming with Jess, Zanna.

"As y'all know, Dad and I gots to go to Walter Reed for rehab. Well, we've just been informed..."

"Today they told us they don't have accommodations for families. Only spouses," Dad said.

"So, we thought maybe... just until I'm

done with rehab... you could stay with Blue."

"I know it might seem like we're abandoning y'all, Zanna, but I hope y'all don't take it that way." Momma put her hand on my knee.

"This could be a blessing in disguise," she said.

"But, you also have the choice to go live with Mamma in Virginia, if that's what you want," said Dad.

"Really? Really? Can Jones really, like, stay with us, Mum?" Blue jumped up and almost trampled Charley.

"Watch it, Jess! And, yes, she can stay with us. It won't be much different from a long sleep-over, but it won't be all fun and games, either.

"I'll need a lot of help with the moving and Charley, and, Zanna, I'll expect you to pull your weight," Mrs. B said.

I didn't know what to say.

It felt too good to be true.

I's afraid if I said anything, the bubble would burst and I'd be headed to Mamma's in Virginia quicker than a slick frog eatin' a blind fly, where the house smelled like dead cigarettes and old fruit.

Then it dawned on me.

"But, when would I see y'all again?" I asked.

"We'll be there for six months, at least. I know it's a long time, Jones..." Dad said.

"So... What about Christmas? And, Thanksgiving? And, my birthday?" My stupid lip started trembling again.

"Oh, bless yer heart, Zanna. We'll make it up to ya, I promise. And, y'all can still celebrate all them things with Blue," Momma said. "All them things."

"And, we can message each other when we're both online, and I'll send you an update by email every week so you'll know what to expect," Dad said.

"You'll know what I'm going through when I go through it. It'll almost be like you're there with us, but you can still be with Blue," he added.

"And, we'll call directly," Momma said.

Blue knelt in front of me like she was gonna propose, or something.

"Please, Jones. Please come with us. Gonza. I don't know nobody in Wyoming. I've never even met me aunt...

"Come to think of it, I've never even seen an Indian before, either." She turned to her mom. "Do they, like, live in tents?"

"You don't know ANYBODY, and they're called teepees, not tents and no, they only use teepees for Pow-wows and other ceremonies nowadays," Mrs. B said, and then added, "at least, I believe so."

"Can I think on it?" I asked Momma.

"Please! Oh, Please!" Blue begged me.

"Heavens yes, child. Y'all can think on it. I know it's a lot to decide," Momma said.

"We thought it should be your decision where you go, since you can't go with us," Dad added.

I stood up, took Blue's hand, and led her upstairs to her room.

I couldn't stop my lip from trembling any longer.

My tears flowed like an old, leaky diaper.

"Why are you so sad, Jones? This is brilliant. We'll be true sisters in Wyoming."

"Oh, y'all wouldn't understand," I said.

But, I knew she would.

She, of all people, would because she lost her dad and now I was fixin' to lose my parents.

How could I tell her what I felt without sounding stupid? At least I'd be with my parents again.

This wasn't permanent.

Not like a box permanent.

"Try me," Blue said.

"Well, it's nothing. I just don't wanna be so far away. We'll be in Wyoming with yer mom, and I..."

I didn't know how to finish.

"Me best friend once offered to share her dad with me. Can I, like, share me mum with you for a while?

"I know it won't be the same, but me mum loves you almost as much as she loves me, and we would have a 'tastic time. I promise.

"If I ever upset you or if you ever feel as if you don't belong, I'll bury me head in dirt for a day. Promise."

The thought of Blue's neck and body sticking straight outta the ground made me smile.

"Gonza! I knew you'd agree," Blue said.

"Mum! She's going to come with us," she yelled down the stairs.

"Wait! I ain't said that."

"Yes, you did," Blue said, and gave me the biggest hug in the Universe. "Thank you. I owe you a big one."

Then, she kissed me on the cheek.

"Eww. Enough already," I said, and pushed her away.

It was gonna be okay.

And, I was fixin' to move to someplace called Wyoming with Blue and her Momma.

"Where's Wyoming?" I asked.

"I don't know," she said. "Let's google it!"

ᴥ Chapter Eight ᴖ
BURYING THE PAST

"What in Buddha's name do you suppose that was today? You know, by the trash cans?" Blue asked, as we lay on our stomachs in sleeping bags on her bedroom floor.

I had moved all my stuff outta the motel room and into Blue's. We decided to be sisters directly. The movers had packed away all her furniture, so we had more empty space than lone peas in a cold crockpot.

"It had a ringed tail," I said, and then sat up in my sleeping bag. "A raccoon! Well... maybe not. If you see a raccoon during the day, it's rabid."

"That's not true. That's just not true," Blue said.

"Google it!" We both said together. She pulled her laptop closer. Blue mashed the keys and clicked the mouse.

"See, here it is. They come out during the day but stay away from people. They mostly come out at night."

"Hey, click on that link," I pointed to the audio file.

The sound coming from the speakers made us both goose-bumpy. It was the exact sound we heard from the dumpster the night before.

"You don't suppose our ghost baby..." Blue clicked some more with the mouse.

On the screen popped up the skeleton of a raccoon, looking very much like our bones in the field.

"Gonza, Jones! We figured it out. It's raccoon bones!"

"Print it out, just so's we can double check it," I said.

We rolled over in our sleeping bags and stared up at the moonlit ceiling.

"How long do y'all think it'll take for Dad to get better?" I asked.

"As long as it takes," Blue said, taking my hand in the dark. "We'll get through this together, Jones. I promise."

* * *

We sat next to the raccoon's bones and compared them to the printout.

"Yep, it's a raccoon," I said.

"I wonder what, like, killed it."

"Well, it ain't no baby, but Hannah could've killed it anyhow."

"Gonza! You're awful!"

"I know," I said. "The wild dogs probably got at it."

We had Mrs. B's garden gloves and trowel with us, and I started digging a pit.

"Put on the gloves," I told Blue.

I dug the hole about ten inches deep.

"That's deep enough," Blue said.

She carefully picked up the bones with her gloved hands and placed them in the hole. I started to fill it in.

"Wait," she said. "Not yet."

She took off the gloves, reached over, and pulled a hair outta my head.

"Ouch! What was that for?"

She held out my hair in front of her and with her other hand, pulled a hair from her own head. She winced, but kept silent. She turned the two hairs, one black, one red, but both coarse and curly, in her hands. She held up the knotted hairs between us.

"There. Now we are truly tied together... sisters." She dropped the hair knot into the raccoon grave and pushed dirt into the hole. I helped.

I mashed the mound down with my hands, making it firm. Blue handed me two twigs and I placed them over the mound in the shape of a cross.

"Should we say a prayer or something?" I asked.

"Here." Blue held out an envelope.

I stared at it, thinking for a bit she had written a eulogy for the raccoon, or something. Then, I realized it was the letter from her dad.

She wiggled it. "Read it," she said.

I took it. I turned it over. My hands shook like a wet puppy in a cat fight.

"Are ya sure?"

"Read it," she repeated. Her eyes were fixed on the grave.

I opened the flap, careful not to rip the letter inside. I took it out. Something fell to the ground.

It was a long, bright red feather. It glowed

in the sunlight. Blue picked it up. She stroked it with her fingertip, while I read:

Dear Bluebird,

I found this feather in the desert today. It reminds me of your beautiful red hair. I thought you'd like it, so I want you to have it.

You know, there's an old myth about a red bird that lives in this area. Every five hundred years or so, the bird is said to consume itself in a fire and a new bird is reborn from the ashes. It's a legend about rebirth and life after death.

They named the bird 'Phoenix'. I think this is one of its feathers.

Bluebird, I don't know what the future will bring. I don't know when we'll see each other again. The only thing I do know is I love you so very much. And, like the Phoenix, we all live on through our love.

Give Mum a hug from me and help her with Prince Charles until

I come home. I miss you more every day.

Remember, time is an illusion, my Bluebird. We will see each other again very soon.

In Love and Light,
Dad

I folded the letter and put it back into the envelope. I handed the envelope to Blue, who stuck it in her pocket.

We sat in silence for a bit longer.

Then, Blue stood up.

She kissed the red feather and put it into her pocket with the last letter she would ever receive from her dad.

She reached out her hand to me.

"Come on," she said, and wiped away her tears. "Let's go have a Wyoming adventure."

* ❧ ☠ ❧ *

The Elementary Adventures of Jones, JEEP, Buck & Blue

Complete Edition

Blue

book 2

Sandra Miller Linhart

To all of the children whose lives have
been uprooted from time to time.

Bloom where you are planted...
but flourish when you're replanted.

To all who've had to start over in a strange place.

Thank you to the Lander, Wyoming of my childhood,
where people were accepting, kind and
unpretentious... And any adventure could be found
in the woods just a few feet away.

The adventure continues to persist...

Sandra

Table of Contents

࿇ ❄ ࿇

❧ Chapter One ❧

A Beastly Stone

We found it in the forest on a Monday after school. It didn't look like much, but it looked like something anyway.

Jones saw it first and, like, dragged me over to it. Her dark, brown braids with multi-colored bands ridiculously bobbed up and down, as usual.

It looked similar to a totem pole without any faces. It stood no taller than me mum. Its uneven surfaces flickered in the shadowy light, which filtered through the leaves and branches of the aspen and pine trees around it.

"Wow," said Jones.

We stood a ways from it, her grip tightened on me arm.

"Gonza, Jones... What do you think it is?"
I asked.

"Glass, maybe. Black glass. Oh, Oh!
Maybe it's that black rock stuff... what is it
called? Obeastian, or something like that."
Jones was doing her 'I-got-it' dance, like
maybe she had to pee real bad.

"But how in Buddha's name did it get
here?"

Jones looked around. "Do y'all think
there's any more?"

"I don't know," I said. And I didn't. I
reached out to touch it. Jones pulled me hand
back.

"What'cha fixin' to do?" Jones was always
the too careful one of us twins.

We're not really twins. That's just what me
mum calls us. And, her name is not really
'Jones' – that's her last name. I could call her

Zanna, because her name is Susanna, but I like Jones better, and so does she.

She calls me Blue, because it's short for Blumenthal, which is me last name. Me mum calls me Jess, because it's short for Jessica, you see.

"I don't know. I just seem to want to touch it. It's, like, humming to me... Do you hear it?"

"Yeah, I hear it, all right," Jones said. A visible shiver ran through her from head to toe.

"It's humming like an electric fence waiting like a stool for a pigeon. That's why I'm thinkin' we should investigate it more before we do nothing else, lest we be the pigeons."

I walked around to the left side of the stone pillar.

"You go that way," I said, and pointed around to the right side. "If you see anything weird or something, scream."

I walked slowly around the large rock. I had a strong urge to trail me fingers across it.

The closer me hand came, the louder it vibrated and hummed. *But, Jones is right*, I thought. *We should investigate. For all we know it could be some sort of electrical rock with a live circuit.*

One touch from that and I'd be a fried banana. And, Gonza, I hate fried bananas. Almost as much as I hate fried okra. Thank Buddha me mum didn't know how to cook that! Jones' momma cooked it for me once and...

"YIKES!" Jones screamed.

"Aaaaaahhhh!" I screamed in reply.

"Gonza, Jones! What in Buddha's name did

you scream for? You, like, scared the bloody Kool-Aid out of me!"

Jones stood directly in front of me. Her eyes were opened wider than me mouth, staring at me.

"Y'all said to scream if I spied anything weird..." she said. "I ain't seen nothin' weirder than you in a long time."

"Oh, Jones, give us a break. You are *too* funny," I said, and slapped me leg. "But looks aren't everything, so there's still hope for you."

"Bonus," said Jones, primping her braids. "So, was there nothin' around that side?"

"Nothing else, but more of the same."

"Yeah, me too."

"What do you think we should do about this, Jones?" I asked, a little too seriously. She smiled.

"I ain't rightly knowin', but I'm thinkin...
I'm thinking maybe we should go home and
google what we can on the 'net. We can come
back directly and take pictures, and maybe
test the soil around it, or something."

"Brilliant, Jones. But, really? Test the
soil? What are you? Loopy?"

"As a fruit," she said, and we raced each
other home.

* * *

"How was school today, girls?" Me mum
yelled to us in the kitchen from the front room.

"Tolerable," I said.

We'd been in Wyoming for only a week.
They transferred our school records from
Georgia and we started right back in the sixth
grade with not much more than a hiccup. We

didn't even get a bloody break, except for the week it took to drive from Fort Benning to Lander. It only took that long because me little brother, Prince Charles, needed to stop, like, every other minute.

"Did you learn anything new?" Mum asked.

"We learned it ain't much fun to be in the sixth grade in a baby school," Jones mumbled under her breath.

In Lander, sixth grade was still in the grade school with the little kids, unlike Fort Benning, where sixth, seventh and eighth grades were in Ray Middle School.

"What was that?" Mum walked into the kitchen with Charley resting on her hip.

"Nothing, Mrs. B," Jones said.

"You learned nothing today?"

"No, Ma'am. I mean, I ain't said nothing much. Um, I learned there ain't but one other black kid in the whole school."

"Does that bother you?" Mum asked.

"No, not really," Jones said. "They ain't mean, or nothing like that."

"Gonzo!" Mum said.

"Oh, Mum!" I rolled me eyes.

Jones giggled.

* * *

"What did you say you thought it was made of?" I asked Jones.

We were seated in front of me laptop.

"Obeastian, or something like that."

I googled 'rocks' and looked at the huge list it brought up.

"Here. Rocks and Minerals. Try that one," Jones said, and pointed at the monitor.

I clicked on the link and up popped another menu.

"Minerals. Minerals. Igneous Rocks...," I mumbled.

"Well, I ain't knowin' what igneous means, but I know it ain't no mineral."

I clicked on Igneous Rocks.

"Igneous rocks... Rocks formed by solidification from a molten or partially molten state... rocks formed by fire," I read off the screen.

"There! That one!" Jones pointed at the picture of a black, glasslike rock labeled Obsidian.

"Brilliant, Jones! I think you've got it!"

"Well, we know what it's probably made of, but still nowhere closer to why someone made it," she said.

"Or, how in Buddha's name it got there," I said.

The corner of the monitor flickered and the sound of a doorbell chimed.

"Hey, look. Your dad's on," I said.

The computer beeped, and a message came up on the screen: *You have a video message from R Jones. Would you like to accept?*

I clicked on 'Accept'. Me face bobbed on-screen for a flash second before Mr. J's face replaced it.

"Hi, Blue. Can I talk with my girl for a second?"

"Sure, Mr. J."

Jones sat in front of me laptop. I heard her address her dad.

"Hey, Dad. Wassup?"

I stepped outside me room.

How many times did I wish I could, like, ask me own dad that?

I felt a lump grow large in me throat. I wiped the tears from me eyes just as Jones bopped her head out the door.

"What'cha doin' out here?"

"Nothing. Just giving you and your dad some privacy. What did he have to say?"

I hoped she couldn't tell me eyes were leaking.

"Not much. He showed me his cool, new arm, though. So... that was nifty as a shiny nickel."

She blinked a bit more than usual. Her smile seemed forced. I pretended to not notice just like she probably was pretending to not notice me tears, and smiled back.

"Neat about your dad's arm, huh?" I asked.

"Yep."

"Hungry?"

"Nope."

"I am," I said. "Let's go see what there is to eat in me kitchen."

❧ Chapter Two ❧

One Brave Soul

On Tuesday, the stone was still there. But, sitting in front of it, about a meter away, was an American Indian boy around our age. I recognized him from school. He sat cross-legged with his back facing the stone. His eyes were closed and he hummed a solid note.

"Blue? He asleep?" Jones aimed her camera at the boy and the strange rock behind him.

He stopped humming, opened one eye, and looked at us.

"No, Jones. He doesn't appear to be."

"Your name is Blue? And you're white with red hair? Aren't you the all-American girl?" he asked, looking at me with both eyes.

"Not really," I said.

"She's from South Africa," Jones explained, and snapped a picture.

"So, let me get this straight. Your name is Blue. Your hair is red. You're white, but you're an African-American?"

"Yes," I said.

"And..." He turned to Jones. "Your name is Jones. You're an African-American, but you're black?"

"Nope," Jones said. She walked to the other side of the stone and took another picture.

"Nope? What do you mean, nope?"

"Nope. My name is Jones, and I *am* black," she said, "but I'm a native American."

"Wait. You mean to tell me you're a Native American - an American Indian - like me?"

"Nope. I'm a native American. I was born in Virginia, like my momma, and my mamma, and my great-granmamma..." Jones said.

The boy jumped up.

"And, you were born in South Africa?" he asked me.

"Yes, Cape Town, like me mum." I said. "And, me mum's mum..."

"You two are too confusing," he said, and started walking away.

"Wait! What in Buddha's name is it?" I asked.

"What is what?" He stopped and faced us.

"This," Jones said, pointing to the black rock with her camera. "This... rock thing. What is it?"

"Grandfather calls it a meditation stone," he said, and turned and walked away.

* * *

"What did Mum pack you for lunch," I asked Jones on Wednesday.

We sat on the end of a long table in the school cafeteria. She sat on one side; I sat across from her. All the other kids sat at the other end, laughing and talking. I didn't mind. I had Jones.

"Looks like peanut butter and... I can't tell. Jelly? Something green. A peanut-butter-and-something-green sandwich. What'd y'all get?"

"Same." I was hoping to trade. "I don't care for peanut butter and mint jelly much," I said, but I'd eat it anyway.

"Mint? Really?" Jones nibbled on the edge. "Not bad," she said, and took a big bite.

I opened me corn chips.

"Did anybody warn you guys about the fish?"

I looked up to see the boy from the meditation stone standing next to where Jones sat, holding a tray in his hands.

"No, what about the fish?" I asked.

"Never, ever, under any circumstances do you guys want to eat the fish here," he said, sitting down beside Jones. "Don't do it. It'll give you stomach cramps. Every time."

"So, why're y'all eating it?" Jones asked, looking at his tray.

"Oh, crikey, Jones. This isn't fish. This's chicken. Chicken's okay."

"Hey, lookit! Chief Blackhead got hisself some new squaws."

A boy twice our size stood behind Jones and our new friend. I recognized his face from homeroom. Three smaller boys stood behind him and giggled.

"Go away, Travis. You guys are stinking up the place."

"What's that Chief? What d'ya say to me?" Travis grabbed our new friend's collar and started to haul him up out of his seat.

"Hey! Hey now, Mr. Blankenship! There'll be none of that!" Mr. Reed, the music teacher, walked up. "Have you and your friends finished eating, Travis?"

"Yes, Mr. Reed," Travis said, and released his grip.

"Then don't you think you boys ought to go on outside and leave Mr. Black and these ladies alone?"

"Yes, Mr. Reed." Travis and his buddies skulked out the door.

"Now then, Robert, is everything okay?"

"Yes, Sir," our new friend, Robert said.

"Okay. Keep practicing your trumpet," Mr. Reed said, and walked away.

"Yes, Sir," Robert said.

"That really yer name? Robert Blackhead?"
Jones asked.

"Not really," Robert said.

He picked at the chicken on his plate.

His face was dark.

"Then, what is it?" I asked. "And, why
did that Travis kid call you 'Chief'?

"He always calls me that, because I'm a
descendant of the Northern Arapaho Indian,
Chief *Wo'teenox*. I'm Robert Elias BlackBear.
Your people dropped the 'Bear' part years ago,"
he said. "You guys can call me Bob."

"I think y'all're brave," Jones said.

"Funny," Bob said, and took a bite of his
chicken.

"Nope. Bob won't do. We'll have to
figure out another name for you," I said, and
took a bite of me sandwich.

Yuck. I forgot it was bloody mint jelly.

"There any more we should be knowin' about the food here?" Jones asked.

"No. 'Cept don't drink the water from the fountains."

"Why not? Will it give us stomach cramps, too?" she asked.

"No. It tastes like dirty metal."

⊶ Chapter Three ⊷

Rehab vs. Rehab

"So, why ain't there more American Indians in school?" Jones asked Bob as we sat in a semi-circle, our backs to the meditation stone, much like we found him the day before.

"Hey! In order for this to work, you guys have to meditate," Bob said.

"Black. We can call you Black. You know, like me, Blue."

"Now, that would be as confusing as Braille on a golf ball," Jones said.

"Yeah, a black girl with a white, red-headed, African-American friend and a 'red' boy named Black," I giggled.

"Shhh. Concentrate on your breathing," Bob said.

I sat quietly, trying to concentrate on me breathing. Me nose began to itch.

"What's wrong with 'Chief'?" Jones asked.

"That's what Travis calls me."

"So? All the more reason to call y'all that. If he sees it ain't bugging y'all, he'll stop," Jones said.

"Because it reminds me of him," Bob said. "He'd just find another name, anyway."

"True. Wankers always do," I said.

"Grandfather calls me *Hono'ie Neeceeebi*, or YoungBuck."

"Then, Buck it is!" I said.

"Hey... don't I got a say in this?" Jones asked, and then turned to Buck.

"Why, again, ain't there more of yer people in school?" She asked.

"Why aren't there more of your people,

Jones?" Buck asked.

"Cuz I think there're only two black families in the whole, entire state of Wyoming," Jones said. "Maybe three."

Buck stood up and wiped the dirt from his butt.

"Crikey, this is never going to work. Come on, you guys," he said, and walked southwest through the woods, the same direction he headed yesterday.

I got up and held out me hand to help Jones.

We ran to catch up with Buck.

"Where in Buddha's name are you taking us?" I asked Buck.

"Most of us go to school on the reservation. That's where I went last year. Then, this summer my parents got sent to rehab and I had to move in with Grandfather," Buck said.

"My dad's in rehab, too," Jones said. "How'd yer parents get hurt?"

Buck stopped walking.

He turned to face Jones.

"What are you talking about?"

"Rehab. Dad and Momma are at Walter Reed Hospital in Washington DC for rehab. That's why I live with Blue's family.

"Dad was in the Army, then he went and lost his arm from here on down," Jones pointed to her elbow.

"A bomb. They're fittin' him for a fake arm and Momma's there to help. He's also fixin' to learn how to walk again."

"Crikey, Jones! That's not the same thing at all," Buck said, and turned to me. "Don't tell me your dad's in rehab, too?"

"I wish," I whispered. Me eyes clouded over, and I felt a lump grow in me throat.

"Her dad died a bit ago, overseas. Kinda

the same way my dad lost his arm, 'cept a woman homicide bomber got him," Jones said, "'stead of a roadside bomb." She took me hand.

"Don't you mean 'suicide' bomber?" Buck asked.

"If she was a suicide bomber, she would've just killed herself and Blue's dad would still be alive, wouldn't he!?" Jones planted her hands on her hips. Her colorful braids bobbed with each word Jones spoke.

Buck didn't say anything. He turned and started walking faster.

We caught up with him at his Grandfather's home.

It was like no house I'd ever seen, even in all the places I've lived. A log cabin stood before us with animal horns and hides everywhere.

A circle of rocks sat in his front yard. It had smaller rocks lined up in the middle, like a sliced pizza, or a wagon wheel.

"It's called a Medicine Wheel," Buck said, "from the Shoshone Nation. Grandfather is teaching me some of the old ways."

"Will he teach us?" Jones asked.

"No," he said. "The old ways are sacred to *Inuna-Ina* - our people, the Arapaho."

A soft breeze pulled at the dozens of chimes lining Grandfather's porch, filling the air with metal laughter.

"Gonza... that sure sounds pretty," I whispered.

"Gets rather annoying in a storm," Buck said. "I'd let you guys come in, but..."

He was obviously upset about something. I felt like an intruder.

"No problem," I said. "See you tomorrow at school."

"Yeah, sure," he said. "Hey, let me know how those pictures you guys took turn out."

He went inside. The door slammed shut behind him.

* * *

"Why d'ya think he was upset?" Jones asked.

"That rehab thing bothered him, I think, but I don't know why it would. It's nothing to be ashamed of."

"Are y'all gettin' anything?" she asked.

"No, you?"

We sat cross-legged in front of the meditation stone, our backs to it.

"Maybe if y'all leaned against it..." Jones said.

"You lean against it," I said.

Jones scooted backward on her butt until her back almost touched the stone.

"Oh, Blue, this is cooler than a polar bear with a buzz cut," she said. "Scootch back."

I scootched.

A warm, tingly feeling bathed me body. I became, like, weak and energized at the same time.

"Gonza," I said. "Let's lean against it."

"'Kay... one, two..."

I touched it on three.

A loud, zipping noise and a brilliant flash of light surrounded me. Sights and sounds and emotions blurred inside me head.

Everything went black around me.

"That's why we don't touch it," a voice said in the darkness.

I opened me eyes.

The oldest man I ever remember seeing knelt beside me.

His white hair hung in two long braids from the back of his head and over his shoulders. He wore a brightly beaded headband. Deep wrinkles creased his tanned face. He chuckled.

"Your kind usually don't see the meditation stone," he said, and helped me to sit up.

Jones was on the other side of him, flat on her back, like three meters away from the stone and just starting to wake up. He helped her sit up, too.

"Grandfather?" Jones asked.

"Well, I'm *Hono'ie Neeceeebi's* grandfather," he said. "What are you two doing on this land?"

"I'm sorry. Are we trespassing?" I asked, rubbing me head. "Is this your land?"

Grandfather chuckled again. "No, *Sitee Hiitonih'inoo*. Land belongs to everyone and everything. However, there are papers for this tract in my name.

"This meditation stone came forth from the Great Spirit for my people many years ago. Long story. I will tell you of it sometime. It is strong medicine. How did you find it?" Grandfather asked.

"We spied it day before yesterday, Sir," Jones said. "We were exploring the forest after school. It just appeared like an old lady at a Bingo game."

"Where do you live, *Noyoot Hiseihihi*?" he asked Jones.

"With Blue... over yonder, across that pasture," she said, pointing.

"You Blue, *Sitee Hiitonih'inoo*?"

"Yes, Sir," I said, still a little stunned.

"Come *Noyoot Hiseihihi* and *Sitee Hiitonih'inoo*. Come with me," he said.

Grandfather headed southwest toward his home.

We stood and followed the old man.

"What does *Noyoot Hiseihihi* mean?" Jones asked Grandfather.

"RainbowGirl, or Girl of Rainbows. Your hair brings me joy. Appropriate name for you, one who wears a rainbow in her hair, don't you think?" Grandfather winked at me.

"Then, why do you call me *Sitee Hiitonih'inoo*?" I asked.

"*Sitee Hiitonih'inoo,* or FireOwner, is a bird of our legends which has red on its head and reddish wings. It owns the fire."

"Wow! Just like the Phoenix," Jones whispered to me.

I touched me pocket. The Phoenix feather me dad sent me was still there.

I kept it with me.

Always.

❧ Chapter Four ❧

Grandfather's Medicine

"Chief *Wo'teenox*, or BlackBear, my great-grandfather, was a brave leader of our people.

"Sometime after Medicine Lodge Treaty of 1868, *Inuna-Ina*, or as your people call us - Arapaho, were told to stay on this land. We would be safe here.

"In 1870, Chief *Wo'teenox* camped near *Popo Agie* River. A group of Whiteman settlers, goldminers, ambushed him. Struck him down."

Grandfather's hands and motions acted out his words as if he was cheating at a game of charades, or something. He emphasized each word he said with a gesture or swoop.

He was as fun to watch, as he was to listen.

"His body rose like a pillar where his life blood spilled," Grandfather said.

"Now, *Inuna-Ina* belief, our custom is that whenever death occurs we do not go back to that place. But, Great Spirit rained down fire rock, encasing Chief *Wo'teenox* in hard stone. There he stands today as meditation stone for *Inuna-Ina*."

Grandfather sat cross-legged. The three of us sat in front of him in a half-circle on the buffalo skin rug in his greatroom.

"It is a good sign for you to see the stone. You must be worthy," Grandfather said.

"What is it you hold dear in your pocket, *Sitee Hiitonih'inoo*?" he asked me.

I pulled the bright, red feather out of me pocket.

"It's the last thing me dad gave me. It's a Phoenix feather from the Middle East. Me dad said it, like, signifies rebirth and life after death. The Phoenix burns itself up and a new one is born from the ashes," I said. "He found this in the desert right before he was killed."

Grandfather took the feather from me hand and stood up. He walked over to the counter and started messing with something.

"Great gift indeed. Appropriate. Phoenix sounds like the same bird as *Sitee Hiitonih'inoo*," he said.

"*Inuna-Ina* give away our most precious belongings. To keep what we treasure is a sin to *Inuna-Ina,*" he added.

I felt that lump grow back in me throat. Surely, Grandfather didn't expect me to give away me feather.

I started to stand.

Buck put his hand on me knee and shook his head.

Grandfather came back. He held the feather in his hand. He had attached it to something.

A small, beaded, worn-leather bag hung from a leather cord.

"It is my Medicine Bag; one of seven," Grandfather said, placing it around me neck. He had woven me feather tightly through the beads.

"One of my most prized possessions," he said. "I give to you."

"What's it got in it?" Jones asked.

"Good Medicine, that's all you need know," Grandfather said, and winked at Buck.

"Did you make it?" I asked, running me finger over the beautiful beadwork.

"No, *Sitee Hiitonih'inoo*. Beadwork is done by *Inuna-Ina* women only. This was my grandmother's. She sewed buffalo hide together. She used the quill of a *Hoo*, or porcupine, to bead it. She carried her medicine in it when she walked on this earth," Grandfather said. "Now it is for you to carry yours."

"Why did the settlers kill Chief Wah-dah... Chief BlackBear?" Jones asked Grandfather. "Did he attack them, or somethin'?"

"One destroys what one does not understand. Whiteman did not kill Chief *Wo'teenox*. Fear killed Whiteman's heart. With a heart filled with fear, man strikes out with the force of that fear. That's what happened on that day. Whiteman struck out with fear. No other reason. Chief *Wo'teenox* lives on, much like your Phoenix bird," Grandfather said.

"Some men think to take a life for no reason shows courage, commands respect. It shows fear... nothing more than cowardly fear. To live among men, to respect life... all life, well, that shows true bravery.

"Now," he said, "you must go. *Hono'ie Neeceeebi* must continue his travels through Kit Foxes *Beyoowu'u* in the Second Hill of Life."

Grandfather helped us up.

"It was a pleasure meeting you *Sitee Hiitonih'inoo*," He turned to Jones, "and you, *Noyoot Hiseihihi.* You are both welcome here again."

Buck stood up, and walked with us to the door.

"What's the Second Hill of Life?" Jones asked him.

"It's sacred. If I tell you guys, I'd have to turn you into a meditation stone," he said, smiling.

"Everything in its proper time, *Noyoot*

Hiseihihi," Grandfather said.

"Even the rainbow shows itself only when the time is right."

* * *

"What do you suppose is, like, in it?" I asked Jones.

I ran me fingers over the beads as if I were reading Braille. Me red feather stuck out from it at an angle.

"Strong Medicine, FireOwner," Jones answered, in a deep voice.

We walked through the pasture on our way home.

"Should I open it?"

"I dunno."

"You open it, Jones."

"No, you open it."

"Okay," I said, but didn't.

"What's keeping ya?" Jones asked.

"I don't know, really, just don't feel like it's time, I guess."

"Everything in its proper time, FireOwner," Jones said, in her deep voice again. "At least now y'all ain't gonna lose that there feather."

"Yes. I guess it is, like, strong medicine. Race you home?"

"Sure!" Jones ran off in front of me.

"Bloody cheater!" I yelled, and ran after her.

* * *

"Is he really your grandfather," I asked Buck at lunch the next day.

The Medicine Bag hung around me neck, hidden under me shirt.

"He's my great-grandfather, one of the last of my family. My parents had two sons. My older brother died in a fire before I was born. My grandmother died in the same fire," he said. "He likes you."

"What about me?" Jones asked. She eyed her lunch tray.

"Warned you guys not to get the fish," Buck said. "He likes you, too."

"I thought it was chicken. He ain't givin' me no bag." Jones opened her milk and sniffed it.

"What is it with y'all? Milk is good food? Only if y'all are a calf with four stomachs, I'm thinkin'." She pushed the carton away. "And, I ain't no calf!"

"Patience, RainbowGirl," I said. "A calf actually has one stomach with four compartments. Eat the broccoli. Broccoli is chock-full of calcium."

"Grandfather never gave me a bag, either," Buck said to Jones. "He invites you guys into his home after school. He said your questions bring him joy."

"Well, if we bring the old man joy, then I ain't gonna say no," Jones said, through a mouth full of broccoli.

✌ Chapter Five ✣

Good Dog!

"Hey, Chief," Travis yelled to us.

We were walking to Grandfather's through the forest after school. Travis must have been following us.

"Hey, Chief! I'm talkin' to you. Have you eaten... I mean, have you seen my dog?"

"Funny, Travis. Why don't you just go home?" Buck asked.

"I'm just here looking for my dog," Travis said. "If you see him, please don't eat him."

Travis giggled like a second-grade girl and ran away.

"That boy's as smart as a razor blade on a popsicle stick," Jones said.

"Gonza, Buck! Why would you, like, eat his dog anyway?" I asked.

"*Inuna-Ina* have a ceremonial dance, a kind of Pow-wow where they boil dog... It's considered a great honor by *Inuna-Ina* to be offered the delicacy of dog stew," Buck said, blushing a little.

"Ewwww. Y'all ain't never eaten dog, have ya, Buck?" Jones asked. I was wondering the same thing.

"Crikey, no! Not that I know of, anyway. But I haven't attended many Pow-wows, either. I just started living with Grandfather. Mom and Dad never got into the old ways."

A shrill sound came from me right. We stopped walking and turned toward the sound.

"What was that?" Jones asked, and grabbed me arm.

"Sounded like a wounded animal," I said.

"I think it was *Beethei* – a Great Grey Owl. They scream like that sometimes, but mostly at night. It must be breeding season," Buck said.

"How did your parents get, like, hurt?" I asked him.

Buck looked at me confused, and then his face cleared as if he finally understood what I was asking.

"They didn't," he said. "They hurt me and the State took them away."

We started walking toward Grandfather's house again.

"How'd they hurt ya?" Jones asked.

"They drank... a lot... and did other stuff," he said.

"Like drugs?" I asked.

"Yeah, I guess so. They never really got over the death of my brother. Anyway, I was... just in the way, or something.

"Grandfather saw my bruises and called Child Protective Services. He took me in while Mom and Dad get help in rehab."

"But I thought rehab is where you go to, like, heal your body and whatnot. Like Jones' parents," I said.

"Well, I guess this is a different kind of rehab, where they try to heal your soul, or something," Buck said. "I really don't want to talk about it, okay?"

"Sure," Jones said. "But, why dog?"

"Huh? Oh. *Inuna-Ina* used dogs to carry their belongings on a travois a long time ago, before they got horses. They honored dogs for their hard work," Buck said.

"So, they ate them to honor them?" I asked.

"Something like that. Crikey, I don't really know. You guys'll have to ask Grandfather," Buck said, as we entered Grandfather's home.

"Ask me what?"

Grandfather stood near the kitchen entrance wiping his hands on a dish towel.

"They want to know why *Inuna-Ina* eat dog," Buck said.

"The same reason we eat chicken, or cow. Meat - nourishes our bodies," Grandfather said. Looking at our wrinkled-up noses, he added, "You people! You think if it's cute, you can't eat it. Dolphins are cute, so you don't eat them. But tuna... tuna's ugly, so you eat it!" Grandfather chuckled. "And, you think *Inuna-Ina* are strange!"

"But, Gonza, dogs are pets," I said.

"Your people make dogs into pets. You do the same with rabbits and goats... and fish. Pigs are pets, too," Grandfather said, with a smile.

"Don't you eat bacon? And, ham? Same thing. Only *Inuna-Ina* do it as Sacred Ceremony. You do it for breakfast."

Grandfather shook his head and smiled.

"Don't worry. I won't be cooking any dog for you," he said, and then winked and added, "Yet!"

"Let me know when y'all do," Jones said. "I'll be sure to be not here."

"Where will you be," Buck asked.

"Don't rightly know," Jones said. "But, I ain't fixin' to be here."

* * *

"Attention. Please. Today for lunch, we have Macaroni and Cheese, Baked Fries, Peach Cup and Chocolate Chip Cookies.

"Teachers, please ensure the lunch count gets to the office by nine with the attendance roster. Thank you. Now please stand for the Pledge."

The bloody loudspeaker woke us up pretty much the same way it had every morning since we got there.

I stood up, faced the flag, placed me hand over me heart and recited the Pledge of Allegiance with the rest of the class, just a little ahead of the voice coming from the loudspeaker.

I couldn't wait for lunch time. Jones and I had something very important to show Buck.

"Mrs. Nelson?" The loudspeaker blared in our room, making me jump again.

"Yes."

"Please send Travis Blankenship to the principal's office."

"Mr. Blankenship hasn't arrived yet," Mrs. Nelson replied to the wall.

I looked around.

Travis usually sits in the way back of the classroom. I hadn't noticed he wasn't there.

"Blue..." Jones whispered. "Blue..."

"What?"

"Do y'all still got them pictures?"

"Gonza, Jones, you saw me tuck them in me tote."

"I know, I just wanna be sure Buck sees 'em"

"When he arrives, could you please send him down?" The loudspeaker squawked.

"Sure thing," Mrs. Nelson said to the ceiling.

* * *

"Did you guys hear about Travis?" Buck placed his tray of mac and cheese next to Jones' tray and took his usual seat.

"Is he in trouble? They called him down to the office this morning," Jones said. "I hope he's fixin' to be in as much trouble as a cat with canary breath."

"I don't know if he's in trouble, or not, but that might explain it," Buck said.

"Explain what?" I asked.

"Explains why they can't find him. He didn't come home last night after school."

"Gonza! We saw him right after school," I said, and almost choked on me french fry.

"Should we tell someone?" Jones asked.

"I already did," Buck said. "I told Mr. Reed Travis followed us part-way home. He's going to tell the principal."

"Do y'all think he got lost in the forest?" Jones asked.

"Who knows? Pale-faced idiot like him could get lost in that small forest," Buck laughed, then looked at me.

"No offense," he said.

"None taken... Redskin," I said. "Ouch!"

Buck had kicked me leg under the table.

"Hey! I have an idea," Buck said. "Do you guys think you could sleep over tonight?"

"Ewww. Spend the night with a boy?" Jones asked. Her nose wrinkled in disgust.

"Crikey, not like that! I have an idea," Buck said again. "You guys think your mom would let you?"

"I could ask her," I said. "I don't know

how me mum feels about us staying the night with someone she doesn't know, though. She'll want to meet you, probably."

"Blue! Y'all got them pictures?" Jones asked.

"You know I do."

"What pictures?" Buck asked. "Oh... the ones of the meditation stone?"

"Yeah. Take a gander at 'em," she said.

I placed the prints from the computer on the table in front of Buck.

The first one showed Buck sitting cross-legged with his mouth opened. A bright light shone behind him. There was no sign of the stone.

"Maybe the flash, like, reflected off the stone," I said.

None of the pictures showed the stone, only the bright light.

"Ain't used no flash," Jones said.

"That's the same thing that happened to the pictures I took. Crikey!"

"That's what I said," I said.

"Nope, y'all said, and I quote: 'Gonza!'" said Jones.

~ Chapter Six ~

A Questionable Vision

"I can't believe me mum said yes."

Buck, Jones and I were walking to the meditation stone from Grandfather's house. Mum had talked to Grandfather on the phone after meeting Buck.

"I think she needed a break from you guys," Buck said.

"Well, from Jones anyway," I said.

"Watch it, Blue, or I'll make y'all pee in yer sleeping bag," Jones said. "Do y'all got a pail of warm water, Buck?"

I stopped walking and held up me hand.

I had heard the same screeching sound from the day before.

"Gonza! What was that?"

"I still think it's a *Beethei*," Buck said, and started walking again.

When we got to the stone, Buck unrolled his sleeping bag. Jones and I unrolled ours.

"I've no idea why we're here," I said.

"I told you guys. I have idea. An idea to find out what happened to Travis," he said.

"Ain't they found him yet?" Jones smoothed out the wrinkles from her bag and situated it alongside the stone.

"No. Now sit on your sleeping bag in this semi-circle, one on either side of me. This time, face the stone. Cross your legs and shut your mouths."

"Wow, Buck, y'all are as bossy as a spoiled blonde on her sixteenth birthday." Jones sat down on her sleeping bag to the left of Buck and did as he said.

I sat on Buck's right. I wondered what was going to happen next.

"In the Second Hill of Life, Grandfather is teaching me the Vision Quest. Now, it's not for girls, so don't tell anyone I showed you guys this," he said.

"Put your hands in front of you, like this." He placed his wrists on his knees, palms up "...and, close your eyes. Concentrate."

"What are we supposed to concentrate on?" Jones asked.

Thank Buddha for me Jones. I wanted to ask the same question, but was afraid Buck would shut me up.

"Crikey! Your breathing! Now be quiet, you guys. Empty your heads."

"That's why the males of the tribe do this," Jones said. "Their heads are already empty."

I giggled.

"Shhhh! Both of you! In order for this to work, you guys have to give yourself over to Spirit."

"It might help if you, like, tell us a little more of what it is we are trying to do," I said. "I feel kind of silly."

Buck opened his eyes and sighed loudly.

"Okay. This is how it goes. I'm not allowed to tell you guys our sacred ways, so you're just going to have to follow me on this.

"We are on a Vision Quest. We sit here until a vision comes to us; a vision that will guide us, teach us, you know?" He looked Jones, and then at me, then closed his eyes once again.

"So, how long we gotta sit here?" Jones asked.

"A Vision Quest can last up to four days..."

"Four Days!?" Jones and I said in unison.

"But, I don't think it'll take that long, that is unless we take that long getting started. Now, are you guys ready?"

"Sure, whatever," I said. "But, Gonza, four days. Give us a break. Me mum will surely send the bloody troops out for us, too."

We sat facing the stone like Buck told us.

We sat there for a bit.

Then, for a bit longer.

* * *

I must have fallen asleep, because sitting in front of me, with its legs crossed was a big, black bear.

The stone pillar was gone.

"*Hello, Sitee Hiitonih'inoo.*" He smiled at me. His lips didn't move, but I heard his voice in me head.

I looked around.

The sun peeked east through the trees at a 45° angle. It must have been around 9:30 or 10:00 in the morning.

"*Where am I?*" I thought.

"*Same place. In front of the stone,*" the bear replied to me mind.

"*Where are me friends?*"

"*Same place.*"

The bear's eyes were warm and brown, not at all scary.

I tried to get up, but realized I couldn't move.

"What's happening?"

"You're on a Vision Quest, Sitee Hiitonih'inoo. Come with me."

"But... I can't move."

"Release your thoughts and follow me."

I felt myself pull away from the rest of me, as if I floated in air. I saw the bear float ahead of me. I looked back and saw me body sitting cross-legged on the ground.

I looked comfortable.

I followed him. The bear took me high above the forest.

"There," he thought-spoke, and pointed. *"That's where we are now. And, there,"* he pointed to another spot just west of the first spot. *"That's where you need to go."*

He zoomed down to the spot.

I followed.

I found myself alone in a part of the forest I'd never been.

An old fireplace stood in the middle of the trees, broken and crumbling. It told the tale of a house that had once been on this spot.

The bear was gone.

I looked around.

The forest was thick in this part. I didn't know if I could find me way back.

I turned east, toward the sun and started walking.

The branches of the trees caught me hair and clothing and pulled me back. The trees surrounded and trapped me.

That's when I heard it, a soft voice in the distance.

"Hey..." the scared voice was weak. "Hey..."

* * *

"Hey...Blue?" Jones voice woke me. "Are y'all okay?"

"Crikey," Buck said. "I didn't think you'd ever come to."

It was dark.

Stars twinkled in the dark sky above me.

The stone stood directly in front of me. Jones and Buck were on either side of me, holding me hands and looking concerned.

"What? What time is it?" I asked.

"I dunno. Ain't much past midnight, or 1:00," Jones said.

"Gonza, that was neat."

"What was neat, Blue?" Buck asked.

He still held me hand. His skin was warm and soft. Me cheeks felt hot.

Thank Buddha he couldn't see me blush in the moonlight.

"The bear? Didn't you see the bear?"

"Nope," Jones said, shaking her head. "All I dreamt of was a beaver.

"She took me to a stream just west of here and showed me a dam she built for her family. She told me it was as sturdy as Stone Mountain, so ain't no worries."

"Wait, Jones! You guys aren't supposed to tell anyone. The vision was for you, alone." Buck said.

"But, since you started... And, girls aren't supposed to do this anyway... I saw a mole, but it wasn't a dream. He took me west, underground to a place damp and wet and hollow.

"I heard an owl screech and the mole told me to listen well. Listen well. He just kept repeating 'listen well' – whatever that means."

"Well, I saw a bear," I said, then told them about me dream.

"Crikey, they're not dreams, you guys. They were Vision Quests. You guys have to know that," Buck said, and let go of me hand.

"What in Buddha's name do we do with them? A bear, a badger..."

"Beaver," said Jones.

"Beaver... and a mole? The only thing they, like, all have in common is... well, west, I guess," I said.

"Then, tomorrow morning we head west," Buck said. "Now let's get some sleep." He crawled inside his sleeping bag.

I pulled mine closer to his.

Jones did, too.

"Doesn't it get cold here at night in October?" I asked.

"It might. If it gets too cold, we can always go to Grandfather's," Buck said.

It got too cold.

❧ Chapter Seven ❧

From the Ashes

We woke up to the smell of Grandfather's cooking.

We were all sprawled out in our sleeping bags on his greatroom floor. The buffalo hide made a comfortable, warm padding.

"That smells as good as hot apple pie in the dead of winter. What is it?" Jones asked.

"Dog." Grandfather winked. "*Hebe, Hono'ie Neeceeebi.*"

"*Hebe, Nebesiibehe,*" Buck replied.

"Did you sleep well?" Grandfather asked.

"Yes, *Nebesiibehe, hohóu.*"

"Good. You overslept the morning away. The noon sun is shining. Or it would be, if the clouds were not shielding Earth from its fire. Come have some hash browns and sausage. The eggs are cooking," Grandfather said to us. "I promise, no dog today. Fresh out."

* * *

"This is 'tastic," I said, and shoveled more hash browns into me mouth.

Grandfather had made them crispy on the outside and soft on the inside. They were the best I'd ever tasted.

"These're the best I've ever tasted, Grandfather," Jones said, speaking me thoughts aloud.

"*Hohóu, Noyoot Hiseihihi.* There are plenty more, if you want them."

"*Nebesiibehe*, can we go for a hike after breakfast? I mean, lunch?" Buck asked.

The digital clock on Grandfather's stove displayed 1:32.

"I don't think that's wise, *Hono'ie Neeceeebi*. The trees tell me it's going to snow. The birds tell me it'll be a hard one."

"Please, *Nebesiibehe*. We won't be gone long, and we'll take the buffalo hides and jerky, just in case."

"All right. But, don't be gone long. If it starts to snow, you head back. You hear me?"

"Yes, *Nebesiibehe*," Buck said. "Hurry and eat, you guys." He put his plate in the sink and left the room.

I wanted more hash browns, but I gulped down what food was left on me plate.

"Thank you, Grandfather. That was delicious," I said, and picked up me plate.

"Yeah, thank you," Jones chimed in.

"In *Inuna-Ina*, we say '*hohóu*' – means the same," Grandfather said.

"Oh, okay. *Hohóu*, Grandfather." I put me plate next to the sink.

"*Hohóu*, Grandfather," Jones said and put her plate next to mine. "Would y'all like us to help with the dishes?"

"No, young ones. You go now, before the snow comes."

Buck came back in the room carrying three buffalo hides and a large baggie full of dried meat.

"Do we have a canteen, *Nebesiibehe*?"

"Yes, *Hono'ie Neeceeebi*. It's in the pantry."

"Here, you guys put these hides on over your coats, and one of you take this jerky. I'm going to get some water." Buck dropped it all on the floor at our feet.

We did what he told us.

Jones put the jerky in her inside coat pocket.

Buck came back shortly with a canteen hung around his neck, thank Buddha. I was getting hot under the buffalo hide.

"Let's go," he said.

He put the remaining buffalo hide over his coat and headed out the door.

"Bye, *Nebesiibehe*. We'll be back soon," Buck said.

* * *

"The sun rises in the east, so we need to go that way," he said, pointing in the opposite direction.

We made our way through the dense forest, stopping every now and then to check our direction.

"How far do y'all think we need to go?" Jones asked.

Buck shrugged, and started walking again.

We walked in silence, letting the sounds of the forest surround us.

We could hear the sound of running water up ahead.

A river crossed our paths, blocking the way west.

"Give us a bloody break! What in Buddha's name are we going to do now?" I asked.

We stood on one side of the river. It wasn't running hard, and didn't look too deep, but it was wide, uncrossable. Especially in the bloody cold.

"There! Look there!" Jones pointed down river.

A piled-stick bridge crossed the river at one point along the path. Except for a small break in the middle that allowed the water to rush through, it spanned from one bank to the other.

"It's the dam! It's the beaver's dam! The one from my dream," she said.

"Vision," Buck corrected her.

"Whatever." She ran down river and stood at the edge.

We caught up to her just as she started to cross, putting one foot tenderly in front of the other.

"Be careful, Jones. You don't know if it'll, like, hold you." I could just imagine trying to explain to me mum how Jones got so bloody wet. Or, worse, drowned.

"It'll hold. The beaver told me. She built it stronger than a horse's backbone."

"Don't worry, Blue," Buck said. "Visions don't mislead. Sometimes they are vague, but never wrong."

"How do you know it was a vision, and not just a dream?" I asked.

Nobody answered. Buck was already behind Jones on the beaver dam bridge.

Jones made it to the break in the middle. She steadied herself and jumped across the gap.

Her foot slipped and she started to tilt away from the dam. Her arms flailed under the buffalo hide, and I thought for a second she was going in, but she caught her balance and went down on one knee.

She grabbed for the branches, knocking some into the swifter running water between the two bridges.

"Jones!" I screamed.

She looked up at me and smiled.

"I'm okay!" she said.

"Thank Buddha!" I said, and heaved a huge sigh of relief.

I took me first step onto the bridge just as Buck got to the opening in the middle.

The beaver dam bridge was sturdier than it looked, and walking on it was easy.

I caught up with Buck just as he was getting ready to leap across the wide gap.

And, it was a wide gap.

Buck jumped. He made it look so bloody simple.

"Come on, Blue! You can do it." Jones stood on the other side of the river, cheering me on.

Buck turned to me and held out his hand.

"Do you need me to help?" he asked.

"No, just give us a lot of room," I said.

Buck took two steps back and waited for me to jump.

The water rushed faster in the middle, trying to escape the wall of twigs and branches. Looking at the water twist and turn made me head dizzy and I started to lose me bloody balance.

"Crikey, don't look at the water," Buck said. "Look at me."

I looked at Buck's brown eyes and took a deep breath and jumped. It felt as if I was flying into Buck's eyes.

...his eyes.

They were like the Bear's in me dream... vision... whatever. Then I felt the branches under me feet and Buck grabbed me hand.

"Well done," he said, and led me by me hand to the other side of the river. When we reached the bank safely, he let go of me hand.

"Let's get on with it," Jones said.

We continued walking away from the sun. The cracking of the twigs and leaves under our feet echoed in the forest. Then, the birds stopped chirping. It grew eerily quiet.

A soft, clean smell filled the air.

"It's getting ready to snow," Buck said. "We'd better hurry."

"How in Buddha's name do you know that?" I asked.

"The snow hushes the forest creatures to sleep before it drops a blanket over them. It becomes so quiet you can almost hear the snow fall to the ground. And..." he sniffed the air. "...it smells like snow."

As if in answer to him, one big fat snowflake floated in the air in front of me, all alone. I stuck out me tongue and caught it. It felt like a tiny drop of coldness in me mouth.

"What's that," Jones asked, pointing ahead.

In the distance, I could see the crumbling, dead fireplace from me dream. The burnt ruins of a house surrounded it.

"Gonza! That's the place of me dre... vision," I said.

"That," said Buck, "is where my brother and grandmother died."

Jones and I spun around to look at Buck.

"Y'all said they died in a fire," Jones said.

"They did. In a house fire. That house. My parents couldn't bring themselves to rebuild on my brother's grave. They've never been back."

"Have you been here before?" I asked him.

"Only in my dreams," he said.

"Visions," Jones corrected.

"Dreams. Grandfather told me it was here," he said. "But I've never actually been here."

Jones walked faster and reached the ruins before we did.

She walked around the big fireplace and disappeared. We heard a big crash and a scream. Leaves swirled in the air above the fireplace. Then, nothing.

"Jones!" I screamed, and ran to where she had been seconds before.

"Be careful, Blue." Buck grabbed me arm and pulled me back just as the ground gave away beneath me foot.

"Listen. Listen well," he said.

The snow started coming down hard, blurring the air in front of us.

At first, we couldn't hear anything. Then, from below, we heard a rustling noise. We got on our knees and tested the earth around us. It was solid until a meter in front of us, then it dropped off into nothing.

Buck and I began greening toward the opening, side-by-side, and peered down into the darkness.

"Crikey! I wish we would've thought to bring a flashlight," Buck said.

"Jones!" I yelled down the hole. "Can you hear me? Are you all right? Jones!?"

I made me way around the edge of the hole, trying to get a better look. The snow clouds completely covered the waning sun. It was becoming harder to see, even above ground.

I leaned forward.

"Jones," I yelled again. I felt me hands slip on the grass and found myself hurling down the side of the hole on me stomach.

Then, the ground sloped more, making it feel as if I was sledding down a mountain. Before I could manage a thought, I stopped on the bottom, cushioned by something soft.

"Ugh," the something soft said.

I stood, and looked around in the darkness. I couldn't see a thing. From above, I heard Buck calling down me name, and I could make out his small head shadowed against the dark white clouds and snow.

I walked up the sloped wall until it went straight up. It was more than likely another good five to six meters to where Buck knelt.

"Blue! Can you hear me?" he asked.

"Yes."

"Are you okay?"

"Other than, like, being trapped in a bloody hole? Yes, I think so."

I felt me sides and me head to see if I told him the truth. I had.

"Is Jones okay?"

"I don't know. I..." The truth is, I had forgotten all about her. "Let me quick check."

I slid back down the slope and felt me way to the something, or rather, someone who broke me fall.

"Jones? Jones? Are you okay?" I felt the jeans of a leg. It was cold. I felt me way up the jeans to her sweatshirt.

Wait. Something's not right. Jones isn't wearing a sweatshirt.

"Rmmmm," the someone said.

I felt me way to the face, and felt something sticky on the forehead. Longish, straight hair matted in the tacky goop at the top of the head.

"Travis?" I whispered.

"Blue?" I heard Jones' voice from the opposite way. "Blue, is that y'all?"

"Keep talking, Jones," I said, and crawled toward her voice.

"Where are we? What happened?"

I found her leaning against the dirt wall.

She had the buffalo hide wrapped all around her. It must have broken her fall a bit.

"We fell into a bloody hole... a well, or something. Are you okay?"

"I think so." She tried to sit up, and then groaned a little. "I'm a little stiff, but I ain't thinking nothin's broken. Nope, nothin's broken. My hand hurts like a chicken stuck beak-first in a meat-grinder, though."

I felt for her hand. I found it, and felt something sticky on it, too.

Blood.

* ❦ ❄ ❦ *

~ *Chapter Eight* ~

Time to Take Your Medicine

"Hold on a minute, Jones. I'll be right back." I crawled back to the slope and up as far as I could.

"Buck. I found her."

"What took you so long?"

"I think I found Travis, too," I said, but to myself I thought, *at least I hope it's Travis.*

"Is he okay?"

"I can't tell. I think his head is bleeding. Jones has a bad cut on her hand, too."

"Blue, do you have the medicine bag Grandfather gave you?"

"Yes."

I felt for it. It was still there.

I pulled it out from underneath the hide and kissed the feather.

"Open it. Pour its contents on Jones' cut and where you think Travis is bleeding. Got that?"

"Yes. Pour the contents from me bag on their cuts," I said.

"Watch your head. I'm dropping down the canteen. Ready?"

"Yes." I saw something flicker above me and dirt fell into me face. I closed me eyes, ducked me head and reached with me hands above me. The canteen bounced off me fingers. The strap caught me thumb as the canteen came close to bonking me skull.

"Caught it!" I yelled to Buck.

"Okay. I think maybe you guys fell into a washed-out root cellar, or something. I'm going to get help. I'll be right back."

I sat on the slope a bit, listening to the quiet. Snow fell through the opening above. It was going to get cold. Very cold.

I made me way along the dirt floor on me hands and knees back to Jones.

"Give me your hurt hand," I said.

I felt for Jones' hand. I placed it on me lap, and then reached for me medicine bag. I took the bag from around me neck. I opened the top and carefully sprinkled some of its contents onto where I thought Jones was hurt.

"What is it?"

"Strong medicine, RainbowGirl," I said, in a deep voice.

I hoped she didn't hear in me voice the fear I felt in me stomach. I had been thinking. It took us hours of walking to get this far. Even with Buck running all the way back, it would take hours for him to come back with help.

"I think Travis is over there," I told her. "Wait here. I'm going to put some of this on his head. He's bleeding."

I started crawling back to Travis, then stopped.

"Jones, do you feel well enough to come with me?" I whispered.

"Yeah, I think." She crawled up beside me. Together, we made our way to Travis.

I felt for his head again, and when I found it, I sprinkled the rest of the medicine where it was most sticky. I put the bag back around me neck and tucked it neatly under me shirt.

"Do y'all think he's alive," Jones asked.

"He, like, moaned when he broke me fall."

"Did y'all finish him off?"

"Gonza, I hope not." But, I feared I had. "Travis? Can you hear me?" I asked.

"Hmmmnfk," came a reply.

"He ain't dead," Jones said.

"Help me put me buffalo hide around him."

Jones helped me lift Travis and completely cover his body with the thick hide as we propped him up against the side wall.

Snow started covering the floor in a white carpet. It made a hollow light against our skin. I held the canteen up to his lips.

"Travis. I have water. Can you drink?"

Travis sipped a little from the canteen and started to come around a bit.

"Who? Where?" He stammered.

"Just two little Indian Maidens come to save yer pitiful hide," Jones said.

Travis fell silent again.

"I'm cold, Jones," I said.

"Here, share my buffalo with me," she said, and snuggled up next to me. "Want some jerky?"

"No, I think we should save it. We don't know how bloody long we'll be down here."

* * *

I saw him sitting in the snow carpet. His fur glistened with the wet snow. His brown eyes - Buck's eyes - stared at me.

"*Nice to see you again, Sitee Hiitonih'inoo,*" he thought to me. "*I knew you'd find him. He is hurt badly. There is fear in his heart. Be careful. The last time one of his kind felt that kind of fear near me, blood was spilled. My blood.*"

"*Chief BlackBear?*" I thought.

"He's back! The grizzly's back! Kill him! Kill him before he eats us!" Travis screamed, fully awake.

"*I must go now, Sitee Hiitonih'inoo. Your Buck has run into trouble and needs my help. Sleep, now. Help will come for you. Don't give up.*" Chief BlackBear turned and disappeared into the dirt wall of the cellar.

"Did you see him?" Travis screamed, and flailed around. Snow stirred up around him. "Didn't you guys see him!?" He sounded like a madman.

"I saw him, Travis. It's okay. Help is on the way," I said.

"I didn't see nothing," Jones whispered in me ear. "What's he goin' on about?"

"The bear in me vision. I had another vision. I guess Travis saw me vision," I whispered back. "The bear said Buck is in trouble."

Me heart was pounding.

If something happened to Buck and he couldn't get back here, we would die here. No one else but Travis knew where we were, which wasn't bloody much help at all.

"Do y'all got yer phone?"

"Yes, Jones, but there's no service here. You know that."

"I've heard y'all can dial 9-1-1 from any kind of phone, working or not, and it'll go through," she said.

"I'll try it." I took me phone from me coat pocket, pulled it out from underneath me buffalo hide and flipped me phone open. It made a *bringggg* sound and lit up Jones' face with an eerie, alien-like green glow.

"What was that? What is that glowing?" Travis screamed. "Is that a ghost!?"

I punched in 9-1-1 and hit the phone icon. Nothing happened. I closed me phone and put it back into me pocket.

"Well, I guess now we just wait," I said. I laid me head against Jones' shoulder and fell back asleep.

* * *

"Where'd you guys go?" Travis yelled, waking me.

"We're right here, Travis. Don't pitch a hissy," Jones said.

"I'm thirsty. And, I think..." Travis started crying. "I think I broke my leg. What time is it?"

I crawled over to him, disturbing the growth of snow on the ground. I held the canteen to his lips. He drank more than before.

"Are y'all hungry, Travis?" Jones asked.

"Yeah, maybe a little. Are you really an Indian Maiden?"

"Sure am," Jones said. She took some buffalo jerky from the bag and put it in his hand. "We took a Vision Quest and were shown the way to you by a beaver, a mole and a bear."

"A bear. Yeah! I seen the bear. Did you kill it? It tried to eat me," Travis said. I heard slopping, smacking sounds as Travis devoured the jerky. "I woulda killed it, if my leg didn't hurt so much."

"Thank Buddha your leg hurt," I said. "If it weren't for that bear, we would've never found you. If you'd killed him, you would've, like, rotted down here with nothing to eat but raw bear."

That wanker, Travis, made me bloody sick. Even though I knew he couldn't have killed the vision of the bear, I felt the sickness of fear coming from him. I knew how Chief BlackBear must have felt toward the gold-miner who killed him.

Pity.

I felt pity now for Travis. Pity and cold.

"Jones, I'm cold. Share your hide again," I said.

"Sure," Jones said, and wrapped the buffalo hide around us.

"Hey, you guys, can I have another piece of that... that meat stuff?" Travis asked.

Jones leaned over and handed him another piece.

"What is this anyway?"

"Jerky," Jones said, and then after a slight pause added, "Dog meat jerky."

"Dog?" Travis made a gagging noise, then fell silent. Soon we heard him chomping on the jerky again.

I don't know how long we were down there with the mad-Travis. He kept waking us up with rants and screams about eagles and worms. We fed him more jerky and gave him water to drink, but we kept our distances as much as possible.

"That's it," Jones said. "There ain't no more water."

"Can we put some snow in the canteen and try to warm it to melt it?" I asked.

"Hey, down there. Can you guys hear me?" a voice came from above us.

"Did you hear that?" I asked Jones. "Or, is it, like, just another one of me bloody visions?"

"Hey!" Jones yelled up.

"I guess you heard it," I said.

"Hey! Is anyone there?" She yelled again, louder. Of the two of us, Jones was definitely the louder.

"Yeah, we're here."

A light darted around the dirt room, blinding us a bit. It settled on Jones' face.

"Dang, do y'all gotta shine that thing in my eyes," she asked, but not loud enough for anyone but me to hear.

Then, the light found me face. I looked away from its blinding brightness.

Travis' face was the next to light up in the darkness.

"Hey! What... what the... Get that outta my face!" Travis screamed.

I heard some voices, but couldn't make out what anyone said. There was a dull thump and the snow swirled around us. Light from, like, ten flashlights filled our hole, and I could see a rope hanging against the wall.

It bobbed and swung. I poked Jones and pointed to the rope.

"Look, Jones, it's dancing."

"No! Someone's climbing down," she said.

I looked up the rope and saw a man in an orange vest making his way down the rope. When he got close enough, he let go of the rope and dropped to the ground. He had a search-light on his helmet, and he shined it on Travis. He took a walkie-talkie from his belt.

Walkie-talkie... what a silly name.

"Roger that. Travis is here, too," he said into it. Then, to us he said, "Everyone okay?"

I couldn't see his face, only the light.

"He's gone as mad as a democrat in an election," Jones said, pointing to Travis. "But, we're cool. Cold, but cool."

We were still snuggled close together, sitting on the ground under the buffalo skin.

It dawned on me maybe we should stand up, or something. I couldn't think right.

"You stay there, while we get him taken care of. Then, we'll get you up top in no time," the bobbing light said.

Jones and I watched silently as they lowered a wire basket into the pit. The man carried Travis to the basket and belted him in.

Travis cried, and wankered on about the bear that attacked him. Then, he rambled on about two Indian maidens who had saved him and fed him dog meat. His voice faded as the basket rose to the top.

When Jones and I got to the top, Buck was waiting with Grandfather. His knee was wrapped; he had a scratch on his cheek.

"What happened to y'all?" Jones asked.

"Long story. I'll tell you guys later," Buck said, handing me back me buffalo hide.

"You saved that boy's life," a familiar voice said. The man who belonged to the voice stood beside Grandfather. His helmet light shined blindly into me eyes. I put me hand over me face.

"Sorry," he said, and turned off the light.

When I could see, I realized the man was Mr. Reed, our music teacher.

"Mr. Reed?" Jones said. "What are y'all doing here?"

"I volunteer as a Search-and-Rescue Worker on the weekends and holidays," he said. He turned to Buck. "Travis won't be giving you a hard time anymore, I guess."

"I hope not," Buck said, and then he put his arms around Jones' and me shoulders. "Come on, you guys. Let's go home. I've had a big enough adventure for one day."

"When are y'all going to tell us what happened?" Jones asked.

"Everything in its proper time, *Noyoot Hiseihihi*," he said. "Everything in its proper time."

◈ Chapter Nine ◈

A Spoonful of Sugar

"So, what did happen to y'all on the way to get help?" Jones asked Buck as we helped him hobble to Grandfather's truck.

"I slipped," Buck said.

"That's it? Ya slipped?"

"Yes, Jones, I slipped. I was crossing the beaver bridge and the branches were wet and slippery from the snowfall. I twisted my knee and went into the water."

"Gonza, Buck, that water's bloody freezing!"

"You better believe it's freezing. I couldn't pull myself up out of it. Then, as I was headed downstream and unable to catch my footing, something caught the buffalo hide..."

"What caught? A branch, or what?" Jones asked.

I could see the bear in me mind's eye reaching out with his forepaw and catching the hide, pulling Buck to shore.

"No, it wasn't a branch," I said.

"No, not a branch, but something. The next thing I knew I was on the river bank and I was freezing. Somehow, I made it back to Grandfather's and you guys know the rest."

Grandfather held the door of his truck open for us.

"Let me take a look at that hand, *Noyoot Hiseihihi*," he said.

* * *

"What was in that Medicine Bag?" I asked Grandfather.

We sat at Grandfather's kitchen counter and watched as he wrapped Jones' hand. The bleeding had stopped as soon as I put the contents of the medicine bag on it, apparently.

Grandfather looked at me and smiled. "Strong medicine, *Sitee Hiitonih'inoo*. Made much stronger by your belief in it."

Jones said, "Well, whatever it was, it stopped the pain as soon as it touched my skin."

"No, really. What in Buddha's name was it?"

"Nothing more than plain, raw sugar, *Sitee Hiitonih'inoo*."

"Sugar! No way!" Jones said.

"Sugar stops the bleeding," Grandfather said, and looking at the expression on me face, he added, "It's good to have handy for a nice cup of tea, too."

He held out his hand to me, and asked. "Can I refill your medicine bag for your next adventure?"

"Yes, *hohóu*," I said, and handed him me medicine bag. "You never know when our next, like, adventure might be."

I looked out the window at the thick, falling snow.

"Or, our next cup of tea, for that matter," Buck said.

The Elementary Adventures of Jones, JEEP, Buck & Blue

Complete Edition

Buck
book 3

Sandra Miller Linhart

To all Native American children, native American children and the children of immigrants of all nations who've legitimately come to find a home in the land of diversity and pride.

May our star-spangled banner yet wave, forever. May we continue to accept and befriend each other, no matter how many towers come down.

United, we stand. Divided, we fall.

"Thank you" to my old friends and inspiration, Robert Elias and Donald Paul, who taught me early on a boy can be the best kind of friend a young girl could have.

"Thank you" to my earliest of childhood friends ~ my big brother, Rus. You taught me the meaning of adventure, where to find it and how to figure out this puzzle called life as we went along. You rock!

And the beat goes on...

Sandra

Table of Contents

❧ ☻ ❧

❧ Chapter One ❧

A Frightening Tale

"How!" Grandfather stood at the stove, facing me. His right arm was up in a semi-salute; flat hand, fingers together with his palm toward me. A huge smile lit up his tanned and wrinkled face. "...do you want your eggs cooked?"

"That joke just doesn't get any funnier, *Nebesiibehe*." I tightened my robe belt and sat down at the breakfast bar in front of the stove. I put my mocassined feet on the stool's foot rung.

"Scrambled, please. Do we have any venison sausage?"

"Yes, *Hono'ie Neeceeebi*, fresh off the deer I brought down the other day."

Grandfather cracked the eggs with one hand and dropped them into the cast-iron skillet, one at a time.

His long, white hair hung in two braids, one over each shoulder. A brightly-beaded headband wrapped his forehead.

He was already dressed in his blue, cotton button-down shirt, and well-worn jeans. His mocassined feet poked out from beneath the hem of his pants. "Will your girlfriends be coming by today?"

"Honestly, *Nebesiibehe*, they are not my girlfriends. They're just friends."

I thought about the past weeks and how, at my new school, I went from feeling like an alien named Robert Black to 'Buck.'

I started sixth grade the beginning of the school year in Lander, Wyoming, after transferring from the Wind River Indian

Reservation when I came to live with my great-grandfather.

Blue and Jones accepted me the first time they met me, and even gave me a nickname. It was a warm feeling and I wasn't about to mess it up by giving in to taunts about them being my girlfriends, or whatever.

Even if the teasing just came from Grand-father.

"And, no, *Nebesiibehe*, I doubt they'll be here. Jones has to go to church, and then she's supposed to wait for a call from her folks."

"Church, huh?" Grandfather put the eggs and sausage on a plate and placed it in front of me. "How's her father doing? Did he get his new arm yet?"

"I think so. Her parents will be at Walter Reed for a spell longer, though. I guess he needs to learn how to use it."

I took a bite of sausage, and said with a full

mouth, "Jones said he emailed her a picture of it. She also said there was a picture of him learning to walk again."

"Doesn't *Sitee Hiitonih'inoo* go to church with *Noyoot Hiseihihi*?"

"No, *Nebesiibehe*, Blue doesn't go to church with Jones. Her mom doesn't believe in organized religion." I took another bite of breakfast.

"But, Mrs. B promised Jones' parents she'd take Jones to church every Sunday while she's in Mrs. B's care. Crikey, this food is good, *Nebesiibehe*."

"*Hohóu, Hono'ie Neeceeebi.* I enjoy making your breakfast. It's been a long time since I had a *Hono'ie Neeceeebi* to care for," he said, and squeezed my shoulder.

"Aren't you going to eat, *Nebesiibehe*?"

"Already did; sausage, two eggs, sunny-side up. *Hono'ie Neeceeebi* needs to get up early to eat with Sages."

The phone rang. I finished eating while Grandfather answered it. I heard him talking to someone on the other end.

* * *

"*Hono'ie Neeceeebi, Sitee Hiitonih'inoo* would like to speak to you," Grandfather said, holding out the receiver to me.

I took my empty plate to the sink on the way to the phone.

"Hey, Blue. What's up?"

"Can I come over? Prince Charles is sick and me mum wants me to keep quiet so he can sleep. I'm going bloody crazy here without Jones."

"Sure. Whatever. We can hang out."

"'Tastic!"

"Do you need a ride, or what?"

"No, I'll walk. It's not too far and the snow isn't too deep. I could use the fresh air, what with my brother, like, coughing up a lung all night long. Gonza, Buck, I almost forgot to tell you. Me mum says we can have a Halloween Party Friday night at me house. Isn't that 'tastic?"

* * *

"Halloween party, huh?" Grandfather asked, as he washed the dishes. He handed me a wet plate. I dried it, put it away in the cupboard, and waited for the next one.

"Yeah. Blue says you're invited, too. What do you think I should wear?" I asked.

"You could wear my Northern Arapaho regalia... you know, the headdress and breechclouts."

"*Hohóu, Nebesiibehe,* but I don't think so.

It'll be too cold, and I don't want to ruin them, or whatever. You need them for the 4th of July Parade and Pow-wow."

"You don't need to be ashamed of our heritage, *Hono'ie Neeceeebi.* We *Inuna-Ina* are a proud people."

"I know, *Nebesiibehe.* I just don't think of your regalia as a costume, you know? Halloween is for costumes."

"You are right. It is no costume. You are too wise for one so young. You must take after your great-grandfather."

"You think? I'll have to take your word for it. I've never met my wise one," I said, and ducked away from the dishtowel headed for my head.

"Go get dressed. Your girlfriend is on her way."

* * *

"*Tous, Sitee Hiitonih'inoo. Hono'ie Neeceeebi* is in the greatroom. Let me take your coat." Grandfather's voice drifted through the greatroom from the front door.

"*Tous*, Grandfather. *Hohóu*."

Blue walked in the greatroom and came to sit next to me on the buffalo hide. Her red hair glistened from melted frost her breath formed in the cold air during her walk.

"Gonza, Buck, nice fire."

"Thanks, Blue. Indian Chief work hard to bring flame." I held up the long fireplace matches.

"Funny. Hey, have you decided what you're going to wear Friday night?"

"Did you ask *Sitee Hiitonih'inoo* if she'd like some cocoa?" Grandfather interrupted us when he walked into the greatroom. He sat down, cross-legged next to us on the buffalo hide.

"No, not yet." I turned to Blue. "Would you like something to drink?"

"Cocoa would be 'tastic, if you already have the water hot."

"'Kay," I said, and stood up. "Can I get you some, too, *Nebesiibehe*?"

"Yes, *Hono'ie Neeceeebi*, cocoa would be nice."

As I walked to the kitchen, I heard Grandfather ask Blue questions.

"So, *Sitee Hiitonih'inoo*, your brother is sick?"

"Yes, Grandfather."

"You feel okay?"

"Yes, Grandfather."

"Your mother does not believe in organized religion?"

"Well, um, no, more like she doesn't believe in fear-based religion."

I could hear the uneasiness in Blue's voice.

I put the cups of cocoa on a tray and hurried back.

"Did *Hono'ie Neeceeebi* ever tell you my story of the *Inuna-Ina*, and how we were made to convert to Christianity?"

"No, Grandfather. He didn't"

"I don't think I know that story, *Nebesiibehe*," I said, as I handed out the cocoa, and then sat down next to Blue.

"When WhiteMan came to the prairies, they gave us land to live and hunt. They called us savages and told us to fit in to the WhiteMan's world; we would be better to learn their ways, their speech.

"Then, WhiteMan found gold and took more land. The Northern Arapaho Nation was sent to live on Shoshone Nation land, on what is now the Wind River Reservation.

"WhiteMan built the St. Stephen's Mission there and sent *Inuna-Ina* children to

WhiteMan school to learn American English. The nuns at the school would strike us if we spoke in our native tongue. Whip us until we spoke WhiteMan words.

"Taught us of WhiteMan's story of creation and laughed at ours. Told us of one God. One God who punishes his people like unruly children. Taught us to fear their God.

"At home, we spoke our language freely, told our story of creation. But, in WhiteMan's world we did not. *Inuna-Ina* believe we create with our thoughts. *Inuna-Ina* believe in reincarnation; that we are all of one, plants, animals, earth."

"Um," Blue said. "That's sort of what me mum believes. She says I'm, like, the master of me own destiny and I create me own reality."

Blue touched her chest where her medicine bag hung.

"Your mother is a wise one. You'd be smart to listen to her," Grandfather said.

"*Nebesiibehe*, did the nuns really beat you guys for speaking *Inuna-Ina*?" I asked.

"Yes, *Hono'ie Neeceeebi*, and WhiteMan thought *Inuna-Ina* ways were savage."

"Crikey! I think I just figured out what my costume is going to be."

"Gonza, Buck, that's great. What is it? Is it really scary?"

"You bet. The scariest." I took another swig of my cocoa, smiled and said, "A nun!"

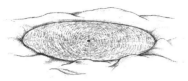

✂ Chapter Two ✂

Little Man James

"Do you believe what your Grandfather said about being your own master, or creator, or whatnot?" Blue asked me on Monday, as I walked up to her with my lunch tray.

She sat all alone at our table.

"Yeah, sure, whatever, I guess. Where's Jones?"

"She thinks she has what Prince Charles had, so she stayed home today. I think she just wanted to spend time on the computer writing her dad. Gonza, it's been bloody wretched without her." Blue took a bite of her apple.

"So," she said, with her mouth full, "do you think we cause what happens to us in our lives?" She again touched where her medicine bag hid under her shirt.

"Why? What are you asking?"

"Well, Jones says that if we pray hard enough, and long enough, and, like, good enough, and if we live a righteous life, and please God, he'll answer our prayers."

"Yeah, so?"

Blue took the medicine bag out from underneath her shirt.

The bright, red Phoenix feather her father sent her was still where Grandfather wove it, in the beadwork of the old bag, which hung from a leather cord around her neck.

"When Grandfather gave me this bag, he said it held strong *Inuna-Ina* medicine. But, really, it's only raw sugar. What is real, and what is faith? What is just myth?"

"But, sugar works like a strong medicine. You saw it stop the bleeding with your own eyes. It's no myth."

Blue's eyes swam with tears and she bowed her head.

"Blue, what's wrong?" I covered her hand with mine. Hers was cold and small. She didn't pull away.

"Well, gonza, Buck! If we create our own reality, and we get what we pray for... I mean, did I create me own dad's death? Was I not bloody good enough for God? Did I not pray hard enough for me dad to live? For him not to be blown up by that... that... bloody murderer?"

Blue spoke the words softly, but tears flowed freely down her cheeks. She held the feathered bag tightly in her left hand.

"Is that why Jones' dad only lost his arm, because she knew how to pray correctly, and she goes to church?"

"I... I... don't know."

And, I didn't.

But, I could see the pain in Blue's eyes and wanted to say something to help her through it.

"Blue..."

I paused a spell, then continued.

"Blue, I think what your dad said in his final letter to you about the Phoenix bird is true. I believe we live on through love and our souls never die. I believe my own brother was reincarnated, and is living a happy life somewhere in this world, or another. I believe I'll meet him someday. I have no proof... no way of knowing, but I believe these things."

"Why? Why do you believe?"

"I don't know that either. Maybe... Maybe only because it helps. That may be the only reason to believe anything, because it gets you through another day.

"Jones believes what her parents believe and what she was taught to believe and it helps her. So, she wants to help you by teaching you what she believes. But, crikey, Blue. She would never say those things to hurt you. You have to know that."

Blue wiped her nose on her napkin.

"I miss me dad so much."

"I miss my parents, too, Blue... but, things happen for a reason. Reasons we aren't aware of. We can't see the big picture. We just have to believe things are working out the way they're supposed to, and we're right where we're supposed to be in this Universe.

"If your dad hadn't been killed in the war, and Jones' dad hadn't lost his arm, I would never have met you guys. And, crikey, I gotta tell you, Blue. I don't mean I'm happy all that happened, but I'm really glad you guys are here."

I felt my cheeks grow hot and I hoped Blue couldn't see me blush.

I took my hand off hers, and took a bite of food to try to ease the awkwardness I was feeling.

"Theoretically, food such as this shouldn't even infiltrate our digestive tract."

I looked up to see a kid sit down next to Blue. He wore blue jeans, a red flannel shirt, and a green tie. He looked like he was in the third grade, or something.

He reached up, slicked down his brown hair over his left eye with his right hand, and then held it out for me to shake.

"Hi. Guess I ought to introduce myself. Name's James Edward Eugene Parker."

"Buck," I said, and shook his offered hand.

He pushed the black-rimmed glasses up his nose and presented his hand to Blue, who just looked at it, and then him.

"What grade are you in?" She asked.

"As of ten minutes ago, I am in the sixth

grade, which, I presume, is the same as you and Mr. Buck."

James withdrew his unshaken hand and examined his lunch tray.

"This is not what I would call viable sustenance. It has more preservatives in it than this tabletop. Is there any... ketchup? Condiment of any kind?" James looked around the table. Not finding any, he picked up his fork.

"You see, it's all very convoluted... er, complicated. Anyway, I tested out of fifth grade just this morning, and now I find myself at lunch with you fellas. Upon entering the premises, I observed the eating and pecking order of this... this... crowd and ascertained... uh determined... the only folks with whom I could meld, being one myself, would be the misfits... in other words, you fellas. So... may I join you?"

He pushed his glasses up his nose again and waited, fork poised to eat, for our answer.

"Um, yeah, sure James. Whatever," I said.

I looked at Blue who raised her left eyebrow at me. I raised my right one back at her. She smiled, and wiped away what was left of her drying tears.

"Nice to meet you, James. I'm Blue."

"I can see that. The question I pose to you is why?"

"Why what?" Blue asked.

"Why are you so blue?"

"No, no..." Blue smiled. "Me name is Blue, well, actually it's Jessica Blumenthal."

"Jewish, huh?" James asked.

"No, not really. Me dad's parents were."

"But, your dad is not. How interesting."

"Her dad was killed overseas," I said, before James could say something to make Blue cry again.

"Well, I guess then that answers both my questions," James said. "And, to answer your question, I am the age of most third graders, but I hope you fellas will find my conversation stimulating... ah, interesting... enough you won't discard of my company."

"We know what stimulating means, James," I said. "And, yes, you can sit here from now on. Unless Jones has a problem with it." I winked at Blue.

"Who is this Jones person? Gawd, this stuff smells awful." James put down his fork. He looked at his plate with what seemed to be sheer exasperation, then snatched up his roll.

He took a huge bite out of it. And then asked, with his mouth so full I could barely understand him, "The leader of this misfit group?"

"Me best girl friend, Susanna Jones. You'll meet her tomorrow, I'm sure. She's sick at home with me mum." Blue said.

"Why isn't she sick at home with her own mum?" James asked.

"She's staying with us for a bit," Blue said, and left it at that.

* * *

"Wait up, fellas!" James screamed across the playground as Blue and I walked toward her home.

I turned in time to see him slip and fall on his face in the wet snow. His books flew from his book bag in every direction.

He jumped up, wiped the snow from his knees, and hurriedly started gathering his stuff.

Blue and I looked at each other, and then ran over to help him.

"Where are you fellas headed?" James pushed his glasses up his nose and sniffed.

He stood about half my size. I felt awkwardly tall standing next to him, so I walked to the other side of Blue, putting her between us.

"Me home," Blue said. "Want to come with?"

"I want to see how Jones is feeling," I added.

"Sure, if you fellas don't object, I find that acceptable." James finished shoving his stuff back into his book bag and held his hand out in a welcoming gesture, as if to say 'after you.'

We walked together in awkward silence toward Blue's house.

* * *

"What in Buddha's name is that?" Blue pointed to a large dry spot in the field in front of her house.

The edges of the eight-foot sphere looked burnt and the long, wheat grass lay crushed in a swirled, clockwise pattern inside the melted snow.

"Looks like a crop circle. You know, Grandfather listens to a late night program on the radio. They talk about these things. Linda Moldy-somebody-or-such talks about crop circles and whatever. I've heard they've seen them in these parts, but I've not." I knelt beside the edge of the circle. I let my fingers trace around the edge.

"Obviously, your grandfather is a very gullible man. This is naught more than either the remnants of a dust devil, or, considering the burn marks at the perimeter, an incendiary thrown at an angle into the brush, instigating flames to spread outward and inexplicably extinguished at this point." James pointed at the outer edge.

"James, if it was from a fire the whole, like, entire circle would be burnt, not just the outer edge."

Blue pulled out her cell phone and took a picture of the circle. "How could a match melt the snow to begin with anyway? And, Dear Sir, there are no foot prints anywhere bloody near here, save ours. Let's just go see what me laptop has to say about this."

* * *

Blue lived in a brick cottage at the edge of the forest, just across the pasture from Grand-father's ranch.

I enjoy Blue's home. Mrs. B has crystals hanging from the windows, which cast rainbows throughout the house, and she's always burning lilac or honeysuckle incense. It feels like a home should.

"I have a disorder," James said, as we entered Blue's home.

"Of course you do," I said.

"No, really. It's called Sensory Processing Disorder, and it causes my senses to be exponentially stronger than most. I usually don't tolerate incense well." James took in a deep breath. "But, this isn't too bad."

"Well, thank Buddha for that." Blue shut the door. "Hellooooo. Anybody home?" she called into the silence.

"Up here," came Jones' weak reply.

☙ Chapter Three ❧

Dorothy's Munchkin, NOT!

"Where's me mum?"

"She had to take Prince Charles to the doc. He's hotter than a June bug in July." Jones put on a sick face and fluttered her eyelids. Then she spotted James and sat straight up in bed, pulling the covers up around her neck. "Who do y'all have here?"

"Hey, Jones. Feeling any better?" I asked.

"I'm fixin' to," she said, her eyes never leaving James. "And..."

"I'm James. James Edward Eugene Parker." James held out his hand to Jones, then snatched it back to his side. "I would ordinarily be honored to shake with you, but given the circumstances, you would concur it might not be in my best interest to engage in the traditional formalities of a handshake upon meeting. What with your infirmity, and all, I mean." James wiped his palm on his pants' leg.

"Y'all are kidding me, right?" Jones looked first at Blue, and then me. As usual, her multi-colored banded braids bobbed on the top of her head.

"No, James Edward Gene Park..." I started.

"It's Eugene. James Edward EUGENE Parker," he said.

"Ha! JEEP! His initials are JEEP! He's just as precious as a cat in the dryer." Jones face lit up. "Aw, Blue, can I keep him?"

"I don't see anything precious about a cat in a dryer. And, I'm not a pet, you know. I can't be kept. I have parents... and six brothers and two sisters, all older, all whom would miss me. Tremendously." James crossed his arms over his chest.

His lips got real thin.

"Oh, oh, oh... Bless his heart. I just messed out what I'm gonna be for the party, Blue. I'll be Dorothy, and JEEP, here, he can be my munchkin." Jones was doing her "I-got-it" giddy-dance in bed, making her covers bounce around and a pillow fell off her bed.

"That's not at all even remotely humorous. I think I'll abscond... um, quickly leave... now, if you fellas don't object. I don't see how ridiculing me is beneficial to anyone, especially me." James re-shouldered his book bag, pushed up his glasses and headed for the door.

He turned back to Jones and added, "I'm pleased you're feeling better. However, if I may say, you'd make a horrendous Dorothy. She wasn't African American, you know."

"I ain't neither," said Jones. "But, Blue is, so she can't be your Dorothy. Please, JEEP. I ain't kidding. Don't pitch a hissy. Be my munchkin. Please."

Jones got on her knees in bed, and pleaded with James.

"What do you mean, you're not African American? Obviously, I can see with my own two eyes, you are. And, Blue is visibly white."

"Nope, native American, but I ain't native like Buck's a Native American Indian. I'm native to America, like Blue's native to Africa."

Jones was sitting on the edge of her bed now.

"Aw, come on, JEEP. I ain't meaning to be hateful. I think yer as cute as a pajama bottom. Please be my munchkin. It'll be perfect!"

"I wasn't summoned to attend your pagan holiday gathering, so the point is moot. Well, nonetheless, it was interesting making your acquaintance. I'll take my leave, now. I know my way out."

And, with that, James was out the door.

"Bless his heart. Do y'all think I hurt his feelings?" Jones asked.

"Well, duh," said Blue.

"He's different, that's for sure," I said.

"Yes, about as different as a white, red-headed, African-American girl named Blue with a native-American black girl friend, and an American Indian boy friend with the last name of Black," Blue said. "Come to think of it, James, like, fits right in."

"Hey! Show Jones the picture you took," I said to Blue.

* * *

"We would, uh, be honored, if you, um, wanted to sit with us again today."

I stood in front of James at the far lunch table. He sat all alone, picking at his opened bag of cheese puffs.

"Is it that Jones girl's intentions to harass me, and call me JEEP?"

"Well, she feels bad..."

"Because I do not require it, you know. I'm persecuted enough as it is. I don't want it from the misfits, as well." James pushed at the nosepiece of his glasses, but they were already at the top of his nose. He looked as if he might cry.

"Um, well, she..."

"It isn't easy being intelligent. People think I'm being presumptuous and insolent, but I'm not trying to be. I'm just... me." And, for a second I could see the third-grader in James.

I sat down.

"Hey, listen. Jones is a Southerner. She's

honest and says what's on her mind. She really is a nice person. Crikey, she didn't say any of those things to hurt you or make you feel bad. Really."

James pushed at his glasses again.

"What's this... this 'Halloween Party' all about?"

"Mrs. B... Blue's mom invited us over for movies and goodies after trick-or-treating. It's a dress-up party, and it looks like it's just going to be the misfits. The four of us. And, my grandfather."

James looked at me and smiled a little.

"You mean it, the four of us. Me included?"

"Yep."

"Do I have to attend as Jones' munchkin?"

"Nope. Not if you don't want to."

"What is your garb... costume?"

"I was going as a nun, but I don't know if I

want to get in the habit of dressing like a woman."

"That's funny. I get it." James laughed too hard and too loud. I looked around to see if anyone was watching us.

They were.

They *all* were.

"So," I said, in a really low voice, "You want to come over and sit with us?"

"That would be the logical thing to do, I suppose." James picked up his sack lunch and headed over to our table.

"Wait, I have a favor to ask."

James stopped walking and faced me.

"You name it," he said.

"Well, the girls have a habit of nicknaming their friends. Like me. They call me Buck. My real name is Robert Black. Grandfather calls me YoungBuck, so Blue shortened it to Buck. The thing is," I put my arm around

James' shoulders and bent down to whisper in his ear. "They've already kinda settled on calling you JEEP."

"Oh, that. I'll acquiesce to it. I find it acceptable. Anything else?"

"Uh, no, that was it." *And, that was easy*, I thought to myself.

I followed JEEP as he bounded over to our table and took his place next to Blue.

"Hello, fellas," he said. "Did you miss me?"

❧ Chapter Four ❧

One Devil of a Dust Storm

"What do you guys suppose it is," I asked. We stood around the edge of the circle after school.

"After y'all left yesterday, Blue and I investigated it on the web. There was as much information on crop circles as the library holds books. It ain't lookin' much like the crops they showed in pictures, but..." Jones shrugged her shoulders.

"Well, I also researched the limited information on my home computer, as well. I concluded no aircraft made this configuration, alien nor military. Reason A being, there is no scientific evidence supporting the myth of visitation by alien life forms, and two, according to GlobalSecurity.org, no military operations have transpired in this area for over three years." JEEP pushed up the glasses on his nose, and sniffed. "If you fellas ask me, it's a direct result of a misplaced spark of some sort, or vortex winds."

Blue walked to the center of the circle and sat on the dry grass.

"Maybe we should meditate, like we did at that stone," she said.

"That was an *Inuna-Ina* meditation stone. Of course we meditate there. This isn't anything I've ever heard about," I said.

"Should we ask Grandfather if he, like, knows anything about this?"

"Ain't gonna hurt nobody to ask." Jones walked up to Blue and held out her hand to help her stand. Jones leapt back when a spark flew between Blue's outstretched hand and hers.

"Ouch! What was that?" Jones asked.

"Static electricity, obviously," said JEEP.

"Whatever it was, it bloody hurt." Blue stood and brushed the grass from her pants.

We started walking toward Grandfather's ranch in silence.

"Fellas, I still think it's nothing more than storm effect." JEEP pushed up his glasses.

"If a storm caused that," Jones said, "it'd have to be stronger than the head bully at Wimp School."

"Speaking of bullies," I said, and pointed to a patch of dormant honeysuckle bushes.

I could see movement and shadows behind the bare reeds. I heard some loud whispers and giggles, then an object came hurling at us.

Then, another.

And, another.

One landed at my feet and softly exploded,

covering my boots with partially frozen horse manure.

"Run! Those guys are throwing horse pucky at us," I yelled, just as one pelted me on the cheek. "Ow!"

I wiped off what I could as I ran toward Grandfather's home.

I looked back to see Travis and one of his friends emerge from behind the bushes. They had more horse manure in their hands and were throwing it at us.

They were laughing so hard they couldn't aim well, so most of it landed well behind us.

We ran until we made it to Grandfather's.

"Did you guys see that?" I brushed semi-dried manure from the shoulder of my coat. "They were holding that crap in their bare hands! What a couple of morons."

"Gonza, that's bloody gross," Blue said, as she picked manure out of Jones' braids. "I thought after we helped Travis out, the bullying would stop."

"Y'all would think so, but Travis ain't just any old bully, he's as simple as Simon's pie. D'ya get it all out?" Jones asked Blue.

Jones shook her head and pieces of horse manure flew everywhere.

JEEP ran over the fence, his hand covering his mouth. His shoulders heaved, and up came his lunch.

Jones walked up to JEEP and put her arm around his shoulders.

"Y'all are gonna be okay," she said, and rubbed his back while he puked.

She reached down and picked up something off the ground.

JEEP's glasses had fallen off and were covered with thick, orange slime and pieces of undigested cheese puffs.

"Hey, Buck. Y'all got a hose or bucket, or

something? I'm fixin' to clean off this boy's glasses." Jones held up the glasses.

Seeing the long strands of orange mucus hanging down made me gag. I had to turn away.

I pointed behind me to a horse trough on the other side of the fence.

"Don't pollute the water," I said, and gagged again. "And, watch out for Grandfather's bull."

"You going to be okay?" Blue asked me.

"Yeah, I just have a really weak stomach." I gagged again.

"Obviously," she said. "Is there someplace I can go to wash me hands before we go inside?"

I pointed again to the trough.

I finally got my heaving under control. I had barely kept my lunch down.

To be quite honest, I didn't want the girls

to see me upchuck and that's probably the only reason I didn't.

"Like I said, just don't pollute the water. There's a smaller bucket you guys can dip into the trough and wash off in it," I said.

"Why isn't it, like, frozen?"

"Grandfather has a solar heater installed on the side. It keeps the water liquid so the horses and cows have water year 'round, and it won't accidentally shock them."

"Gonza! Has that ever happened?"

"Yeah. A couple of winters ago the sump heater got a short in it when a horse played with the cord. It electrocuted two of Grandfather's palominos; one not much older than a colt."

"That's sad," Blue said, and walked over to where Jones was cleaning off JEEP's glasses.

JEEP had finished revisiting his lunch and was cleaning up next to Jones.

"Sorry about that, fellas. As I stated, this... this disorder... it instigates my senses to overload. The experience of the manure when it struck me was in excess, but then the odor transported me over the perimeter. That might not be the final time you fellas observe me regurgitating my fare. I anticipate it's not too revolting."

JEEP took the glasses Jones held out to him. "Thanks, Jones."

"Ain't nothing."

"No, I mean I appreciate the benevolence, not just the superb handing and cleaning of my spectacles. I didn't dare consider you fellas were keen on me."

"As keen as a puppy to a bone," Jones said, and gave JEEP a little hug.

"Speaking of puppies," JEEP said, as he put on his glasses. "I have yet to ascertain why your Grandfather doesn't possess any canines for protection. It is the most obvious choice for this substantial land."

"He'd just eat 'em," I said, and laughed at the look on JEEP's face.

He was starting to turn green again.

"Y'all don't even want to know." Jones put her arm around JEEP's shoulders and led him through Grandfather's door.

* * *

Grandfather examined the picture in Blue's phone.

"Reminds me of the *Inuna-Ina* story of the Star Husband. Did I ever tell you, *Hono'ie Neeceeebi?*"

"No, *Nebesiibehe*, I don't recall ever hearing it," I said.

"Years ago, when man and animal were true brothers, a group of maidens searched for kindling around their camp-circle.

"One beautiful maiden saw a porcupine, or *Hoo*, near a cottonwood tree and decided it would make fine quills for needles. She determined she would catch the *Hoo*, and ran after it.

"The *Hoo* ran around the trunk of the tree, eluding the maiden. Then, finally, it started to climb. The maiden climbed after it, more determined to trap it.

"The maiden followed the *Hoo* all the way up to the top of the tree, never able to get close enough. She looked down and saw her friends as tiny specks below her, beckoning her to come down out of the tree.

"But, the *Hoo* sat on the topmost branch of the cottonwood and the maiden knew she would claim her prize soon.

"As she reached the top, the tree grew all the way to the stars, and the *Hoo* scampered up. The maiden was still determined to have the perfect quills, so she continued after the *Hoo* until she reached the edge of the sky, above the stars. She climbed out onto the ground above the stars, where the *Hoo* sat waiting for her.

"The *Hoo* took the maiden into his camp-circle where his father and mother lived. They welcomed her and furnished her with the very best. A lodge was put up for the maiden and the *Hoo* to live as husband and wife.

"The *Hoo* supplied the maiden with buffalo hide and food. He cautioned her to not dig too deep with the digging stick while in search of roots, and to come home early when out for a walk.

"One day, after the maiden finished her work at home, she went out in search of potatoes. She carried with her the digging stick. She found a thick patch and started digging. She wanted to fill her basket.

"She accidentally struck a hole, which surprised her very much. She looked down into the hole and saw the green earth and her old camp-circle below. She carefully covered the spot and marked it.

"The maiden saved sinew from each buffalo the *Hoo* brought her, and hid it under her robes so as not to cause suspicion among the elders.

"Early one morning, after her husband left for more meat, she took the digging stick and the sinew back to the thick patch. She tied the sinew together to form a long rope.

"She fastened one end to the digging stick and the other end around her waist. She placed the digging stick across the hole and lowered herself down toward the earth.

"But, the rope wasn't long enough, and she found herself suspended above the top of the cottonwood, but not near enough to possibly reach it."

Grandfather paused to take a sip of his coffee.

"Gonza! Why would a maiden marry a porcupine?" Blue asked.

"Yeah, sounds like a prickly situation, if y'all ask me," Jones added.

Grandfather looked at us with a slight smile. He took another sip of his coffee.

"Y'all ain't gonna leave us hangin' like that there maiden, are ya?" Jones asked.

JEEP popped to his feet. He walked over to his coat. "Well, fellas, I must depart. No disrespect intended, Grandfather, but I'm not precisely certain why our circle made you reminisce about a maiden who married a porcupine, but... whatever."

"Wait, JEEP! Ain't ya gonna stick around to find out?"

"Negative, Jones. I'm convinced my family is speculating where I am. I'm also confident this folktale has little to no bearing on our research."

"Are you sure, young one?" Grandfather asked. His deep voice was soft, but his words echoed in the greatroom.

"Many times we learn great truths from our ancestors and the stories they tell. Did you find a smooth, flat rock in the center of your circle?"

JEEP turned to face Grandfather. "I don't recollect distinguishing a stone of any roughness in the core, but then again, I wasn't expecting one."

"Maybe you should," Grandfather replied, and took another sip of his coffee.

৯৯ 👽 ৫৫

❧ Chapter Five ❧

No Stone Unturned

I stood in the middle of the circle and looked out. A strange vibration started at my feet and worked its way up my legs. I didn't know if it was just my imagination, or not, but I quickly stepped away from the center anyway.

"Hey! Buck!"

I looked in the direction of my name being called and saw Jones and Blue walking toward me, their book bags on their backs.

"Hey, you guys. Good morning."

"Did y'all find a rock?" Jones asked as she approached.

"Not yet, but I just got here. Haven't had a

chance to look." I hunkered down and felt through the bent grass. I experienced the same vibration and yanked my hand away.

"Gonza, Buck. You okay?"

"Uh, yeah... I just... never mind." I carefully felt around the center again. The tip of my pinky touched something hard and warm.

"Hey, there's something here," I said, and set my book bag down so I could use both hands. I felt around and came up with a smooth, flat, black stone, about the size of a potato. It felt hot. I tossed it to Jones.

"Careful," she said, then added, "Oh! That's as warm as a baby's bottom in a newly dirtied diaper. The sun, y'all think?" She tossed the stone to Blue.

"What? You fellas playing a stone-aged version of hot potato?" JEEP entered the circle.

I hadn't seen nor heard him coming. He had an annoying habit of popping in and out like that.

Blue tossed the stone to him. "Sure, your turn."

"Wow! I didn't consider the sun to be that luminous yet, however black does absorb heat. Speaking of the sun, I can ascertain by its position in the atmosphere, our time is truncated. Meaning, we're going to be late for school."

JEEP tossed the stone to me. I dropped it into my book bag.

* * *

"Have you guys decided what you're going to be for Halloween?" I asked, as we sat at lunch.

The black stone lay on the table in front of us. We all kept our eyes on it, as if it was going to start jumping, or whatever.

"I'm still thinking we should go as Dorothy and her munchkin," Jones said to JEEP.

"No way. Not even an option," he said.

"Well. I'm going as Dorothy, anyways."

"Anyway," JEEP said.

"Anyway, what?"

"It's anyway, not anyways. You don't say 'anyhows', do you?"

"Anyway, anyways... What dif does it make?" Jones picked up her lunch tray and stomped over to the trash can.

"Anyway..." I said, and picked up the rock. I turned it over in my hand. It still felt warm. "What are you going as, Blue?"

"Haven't decided," Blue said, and picked up her tray. "Me mum's going to help me think of something tonight. It's getting bloody close. The party is in, like, two days." She walked over and deposited her uneaten lunch in the garbage can. She and Jones walked back to the table.

"Why are you fellas so despondent?" JEEP asked, and rolled his paper sack up in a ball.

He had started bringing his lunch in a sack the last couple of days. So far, he always brought the same thing: half an apple, bag of cheese puffs and a chocolate bar. He had a small carton of soy milk - sometimes chocolate, sometimes vanilla.

JEEP had explained he's also lactose intolerant and can't drink milk.

Go figure.

"If I was knowin' what that word meant I might be answering y'all," Jones said.

"Means downhearted," said JEEP.

"Must be the weather," Blue said.

The snow fell in big flakes outside the lunchroom windows.

I shivered.

* * *

"Do y'all think the snow covered the circle?" Jones adjusted her neck scarf.

The school bell had rung and we were on our way outside. The snow hadn't let up all afternoon; our feet disappeared into the white ground as we headed for home.

"Hey, fellas. I had better go straight home," JEEP said. "I wouldn't want to get caught up in a nasty snowstorm. Call me later, if you desire, or... I guess I'll see you fellas tomorrow." And, with a little salute, JEEP headed off in the other direction.

"Bye, JEEP. See ya tomorrow," Jones called after him.

"Yeah, see you," I said, as Blue waved silently to his back.

"It looks as if the snow's going to get bloody deep tonight," Blue said.

We trudged through the snow, leaving a trail of foggy footprints behind us. When we came to the circle, we stopped and stared in silence for a spell.

As the snow around the circle got deeper, the edges of the circle remained crisp and intact. Steam floated up from the smashed-flat grass.

"Maybe it's from something internal... you know, as if something is buried under there that, like, gives off heat or something." Blue shifted her book bag from one shoulder to the other.

"I ain't knowin', but it gives me the creepy-jeepies," Jones said. "Let's get."

I didn't say anything, but I could swear I felt the stone in my book bag burning a hole in my back.

We walked in silence to Blue's home.

"See you guys tomorrow," I said.

"Ain't ya coming in?" Jones stomped the dry snow off her boots and brushed at Blue's shoulders and hat.

"Naw, not this time. Something feels weird out."

"All right," Blue said. "Be careful walking. It's starting to get bloody dark out."

"Sure."

"Call us when you get home," Blue said.

"Yeah. I feel the weird, too," Jones added.

I turned and headed down the walk. No sooner had I heard the door shut behind me, a streak of white light lit up the darkened sky. It formed a ball and hovered over Grandfather's ranch. A reddish-orange beam of light blipped from the bottom.

I rubbed my eyes and looked again.

It flashed brightly and disappeared.

"Did you guys see th...?" I turned back to see I was standing alone in Blue's front yard. I looked again at the sky above Grandfather's ranch and saw nothing out of the ordinary. The snow fell silently.

Except for the trail of bright green behind my eyelids when I closed my eyes, like an imprint of a camera flash, I would have never believed I saw anything.

I ran toward Grandfather's home.

I got almost completely through the field when I spotted Grandfather's prize bull lying on the ground next to the water trough.

Steam rose from its body. A strange chemical-type smell surrounded the still body of the bull.

"*Nebesiibehe*!!" I screamed through the silence. "*Nebesiibehe*!! Come quick! I think the bull got shocked."

"What is it, *Hono'ie Neeceeebi*?" Grandfather emerged from the house, wiping his hands on a dishtowel.

He saw me standing next to his bull and came running toward me. He knelt down in the snow next to the bull. "I haven't seen anything like this since the summer of 1976."

"Like what, *Nebesiibehe*?"

"See, here. Look where the bull is. There are no tracks, no prints leading up to this carcass. Except yours and mine. But the snow has... has poofed... yes, good word, poofed up like the bull was dropped from height of maybe two... three feet in the air." Grandfather stood and walked around the bull.

"And, see, here, where the parts of bull have been surgically cut away... almost burnt, cauterized. No blood. No blood anywhere. And, he's missing his eyes. And, his eyelashes."

The white snow all around showed no

signs of blood anywhere, not even under the large animal. A shiver ran up my spine and I took a step back.

The smell rising from the dead animal made me gag. Grandfather took his Leatherman tool from his belt and opened the knife blade. He knelt, and plunged the knife in and out of the bull's neck easily, but no blood spilled from the wound.

"What does that mean, *Nebesiibehe?*" My hand still covered my mouth.

Grandfather stood up and looked into the sky, as if searching. Then he looked at the bull again. He walked to the other side and pulled at the bull's leg.

"See, here. Clamp marks. On all four legs. Like he was hung from somewhere." Grandfather looked up into the sky again.

"Did you see anything before you found him? Hear anything?" He asked me.

I just stood there and looked at Grandfather.

He waited. Then, finally, I spoke. "What... what do you mean? Like what?"

"Anything strange? Out of the ordinary?" Grandfather's eyes pierced mine. "Right before I heard you call my name... maybe five or so minutes ago, the lights browned-out in the house. I thought the snow weighed too thick on the power lines. What do you think, *Hono'ie Neeceeebi?*"

Grandfather put the Leatherman back in its holster, rubbed his hands on the towel, and stared at me. I wanted to tell him of the light in the sky. But something kept me from speaking up.

"I... I don't know what you mean," I said, as I watched the last of the heat rise from the bull in a wisp of vapor.

ꝏ 👽 ꝏ

❧ Chapter Six ❧

I Suspect

"In 1976, we had a bunch of cattle done like that on this land. Right before we found them, I saw strange lights in the sky. Never told anyone. Didn't think they'd believe me.

"Other ranchers in the area and as far away as Colorado and New Mexico, Kansas, Idaho, I think, all over – people say they saw strange lights and then their livestock were done like that. Lost, oh, I'd say about 10,000 head of cattle in these areas by 1979. Never got any answers either."

Grandfather handed me a cup of hot cocoa and sat down on the floor next to me in the greatroom.

I leaned over and put another log on the fire. I took a sip of cocoa.

The warmth of both the fire and the cocoa eased me a bit. We waited for the sheriff.

"What if... What if I think I may have seen something?" I said.

Grandfather put down his cup. He patiently waited for me to continue.

"I mean... What if I might have thought I saw something in the sky above the house right before?"

"Like a beam of reddish-orange light? A flash?" Grandfather asked.

"Yeah, maybe. I think so. I really can't remember now."

The sharp knock on the door made us both jump.

* * *

"You say the boy actually found him?"

The sheriff's deputy held a pad of paper in his hand and took notes. His name badge read BLANKENSHIP.

"Yes. Robert found the bull on his way home from school."

"And, basically he didn't hear or see anyone coming or going?"

Grandfather hesitated.

"No. He said he didn't see anyone or hear anyone."

"That true?" Deputy Blankenship stopped writing and looked at me with an icy stare.

"Uh, yeah. That's true. No person around that I could see or hear." I felt he knew I was holding something back.

"It was snowing pretty hard, though and the skies were very dark, too," I added.

"Well, basically I'll file this report and talk to the neighbors and get back to you later. In the meantime, I'll have the animal control officer basically come pick up the carcass and actually take it to the vet. He can maybe figure out what literally caused that chemical smell around the bull.

"Basically, if there's actually any funny business going on here, we'll literally know soon enough." The deputy flipped his little notebook closed with a snap and eyed me again.

"Anything more you want to add to your statement, son?"

"No... No, Sir. Not that I can think of, anyway."

"Okay, Mr. Black. We'll be in touch." Deputy Blankenship walked out, then hesitated at the door, and turned back to Grandfather.

"Are you teaching the boy your Indian ways? Basically, the hills of life and stuff?" He asked.

"Yes, I am," Grandfather said.

The deputy nodded, and shut the door behind him as he left.

"Shouldn't we have said anything about the lights?" I asked.

"No. Too soon. I need you to tell me more. If there's anything I think can help them in their investigation, I'll let them know. In the meantime, I think it's best they think we're mentally stable."

"You think I'm crazy?!"

"No, *Hono'ie Neeceeebi*, I don't. But people don't like strange talk, and they like people who talk of strange things even less. The less said the better, for now, I think."

Grandfather sat back down on the greatroom floor and picked up his cocoa.

"Now, then. Tell me again exactly what you remember seeing. Start from leaving the school with your friends."

I took a sip of cocoa, and began talking.

* * *

"Sheriff's deputies aren't sure what Northern Arapaho ritual was portrayed in the slaying of Mr. Black's prize bull tonight, but Deputy Tom Blankenship had this to say..."

The blonde woman on TV froze her smile and waited for the clip of Deputy Blankenship to begin. The television screen flashed to the man who had been standing in Grandfather's house just hours before.

"Actually, it was quite evident that the bull had basically been stabbed in the neck and all the blood had literally been drained from the animal. For what purpose, of that we are not aware. Be that as the case may be, basically a resident of the ranch is actually our main and only suspect.

"The troubled adolescent appears to be actually learning ancient Indian tribal rituals. Basically, his parents have actually been in trouble with the law and are, in fact, literally in rehab for drugs and alcohol abuse.

"Because of that, the boy is basically in the custody of his great grandfather at the Black Ranch. I cannot divulge any more information while this investigation actually remains opened."

The clip of the deputy blipped off and the blonde woman reappeared.

"Deputy Tom Blankenship went on to say that charges are pending against the adolescent residing at the Black Ranch. This is Danna Diamond, KETV News, channel 2."

Grandfather turned off the television and sat silently.

"*Nebesiibehe*, what did they mean by 'troubled adolescent'? Do you think they have a suspect?"

"I suspect they suspect it was you, *Hono'ie Neeceeebi*."

* * *

"Gonza, Buck! Why didn't you tell us?" Blue looked up from her lunch tray at our table as I walked up to them.

I sat down across from her, next to Jones.

"Nothing to tell, really," I said, and pretended to examine my peas.

"Nothing to tell! Gonza! That's not what I heard. Travis is, like, blabbing all over the school how you killed your grandfather's prize bull and drank its blood for some ancient tribal custom or ritual. He said his dad told him all about it."

"How would his dad kn...?" *Oh, Deputy Blankenship... Travis' last name is Blankens...* It became all very clear to me.

"Pretty barbarian, if you ask me."

As usual, JEEP popped in out of nowhere with a sack lunch in hand and sat down next to Blue.

"Drinking the tepid blood of a dead bull, what with Mad Cow disease running rampant throughout the world... kinda creepy, yet somewhat apropos for Halloween, too."

"I did not drink the blood of that bull, or any other!" I got up and dumped my uneaten food in the trash.

As I hurried toward the door, I heard Jones call to me.

"Hey, Buck. Wait up!"

I didn't.

I pushed open the door of the lunchroom. I needed to get to the bathroom.

I could feel my cheeks getting hot. I knew it was only a matter of time before the tears in my eyes spilled out onto my face. I didn't want anyone to see that.

"Hey, Chief... Hey, Chief! I'm talking to you."

I ducked into the bathroom, and entered the far stall against the wall.

I sat on the toilet.

"Hey, Chief. I seen ya come in here. What ya running from? You ain't getting away from me."

I heard Travis enter the bathroom. "Are ya ascared of me 'cuz I ain't no dumb animal?"

I wasn't too sure about him not being a dumb animal, but I kept quiet.

"Like that there bull you kilt? Wassa matter, Chief Crazy Bull?"

I heard the bathroom door swing open again. For a split-second, I thought Travis had gone away.

"Mr. Blankenship? Why don't you just vacate the vicinity before something bad happens to you?" JEEP's little voice barely made it under the stall.

I had to strain to hear him.

"What'cha gonna do, Runtface? Ooooo, I'm so ascared."

"I have to warn you, Mr. Blankenship, or may I call you Travis?"

JEEP continued talking without waiting for his answer.

"Travis, I am required to equip you with the knowledge I am qualified in the arts of Taekwondo, Reiki and Yoga. Mastered them all by the age of two.

"So, if you'd prefer to remain mobile and upright for the rest of the day, I highly recommend you vacate the premises."

"You think I'm ascared of you and your big words, Runtface? Gruntface?"

I heard a strange slapping sound, and then a loud thud.

Then, someone was knocking lightly on the stall door.

"Are you in there, Buck? The girls and I want to extend our apologies for our blatant insensitivity."

I opened the door and looked over JEEP's head to the pile on the floor that was once Travis.

"How did you... What did...?"

"I tried to explain to him. Mastered!" JEEP pushed up his glasses, turned and walked to the door, stepping over Travis' splayed body on his way. "Coming?"

"Yeah... just a sec." I leaned over Travis' body and saw his chest rise up and down.

"He'll be fine, aside from the migraine he'll have. Vulcan death grip, you know. Out like a light," JEEP assured me.

"I didn't know you were a Star Trek fan," I said, as I stepped over Travis' body and followed JEEP out the door.

"Name one brainiac who isn't."

"What did you say you were mastered in?"

"Taekwondo, Reiki, and Yoga."

"Crikey! That's pretty impressive. I know what Taekwondo is, but what're Reiki and Yoga? Just other types of martial arts?"

"Naw. Reiki is the fru-fru art of holistic healing through touch – hands-on, if you will, and Yoga is more of a stretching exercise... keeps me limber." And with that, JEEP did a back flip in the middle of the hall.

"You're one amazing kid. Did anyone ever tell you that?"

"Yeah, my parents. Every day of my life,"

JEEP said, and pushed up his glasses. His face disappeared behind his smile. "They call me their Indigo Child."

❧ Chapter Seven ❧

Fallen Star

"Sources close to the accused tell us he was acting weird just moments before the incident."

Danna Diamond's voice stopped short when Jones pressed the power key on the remote.

"Smarmy news reporters! She done changed my words around. What I said was: 'It was weird out.'"

Jones dropped the remote on the buffalo hide rug in Grandfather's greatroom.

"You talked to her? You guys talked to her about me?"

I had come home early from school because everyone had been giving me such a hard time. Travis hadn't missed anyone with his gossip and lies.

Jones, Blue, and JEEP came over after school to check up on me.

"Gonza, Buck, she was right there after school. It was as if someone had told her who your friends are and she bloody swooped down on us. Thank Buddha you weren't there."

"Yeah, like a bumblebee to a flower, she done swooped down. I weren't thinking she'd twist my words all up like a pretzel. I was just trying to tell her how weird it felt out, and all," Jones added.

"And, Gonza, Buck, it did feel weird out yesterday afternoon, you know?"

"I know," I said.

"Explain weird," JEEP said.

"Weird... you know, supernatural, eerie. Didn't you feel something, like, strange on your way home, JEEP?" Blue asked.

"Well, except for the meteoroid that streaked through the skies just as I was entering my domicile... no, not really thinking that's weird. Pretty much normal sky activity for the Orionid Meteor showers, not that they're visible to many. And the Leonid Meteor showers don't really begin for a few weeks yet, but..."

"Well, we all..." Jones began.

"Wait! JEEP, what did you just say?" I grabbed his arm.

"Ow, Buck! That hurts. Let go!" JEEP tried to pull away from my grasp. "Let me go!"

"Sorry." I released his arm. "I didn't mean to... but, what did you say? You saw a meteorite?"

"No, what I said was I saw a meteoroid." JEEP massaged his arm. "A meteorite is the part that one finds on the ground of what is left after the meteoroid makes it through the atmosphere. The streak one sees, or meteor, as it enters our atmosphere is the phenomenon I observed."

JEEP pushed his glasses up his nose and stood up.

"Hey! I just deciphered the origin of your so-called crop circle. Who has that stone you fellas found in the epicenter of that circle?"

"So, you did find a rock?" Grandfather came into the greatroom with a tray of hot cocoa, and a cup of coffee for himself.

"Yes, *Nebesiibehe*, I forgot to tell you, what with all this bull stuff going on."

"May I see it?" Grandfather put the tray in the middle of our circle and sat down with us.

"It's in my book bag. In my room. Hold on." I ran to my room to get it.

* * *

Grandfather turned the warm stone over in his hand and rubbed his thumb over the smooth surface.

"So, we left our maiden swinging from the stars on a buffalo sinew rope, didn't we?" Grandfather took a sip of coffee.

"Yes, Grandfather," Blue said, and picked up a cup of cocoa.

"Well, now, the time came that the *Hoo* became worried and went out searching for his missing bride. He found the stick across the hole and looked down upon the earth. He saw the beautiful maiden hanging there, above the trees. He picked up a flat stone and hurled it at the girl. It missed her and because he threw it hard, it caught fire on the way down. He hurled another one and the same thing happened. Then, the *Hoo* thought to himself: *'Well, the right thing to do is to see her touch the bottom.'*

"With that, he picked up a flat, black stone and said: 'I want this stone to light on top of her head,' and he dropped it carefully through the hole along the sinew rope.

"It struck the top of her head and broke the rope, and landed her safely on the ground. She picked up the stone and returned to the camp-circle of her family."

Grandfather held up the stone.

"And, that, my young ones, is the *Inuna-Ina* explanation of meteor showers."

"Gonza, Grandfather. So, what you're saying is that this stone is a meteorite?"

"Could be, *Sitee Hiitonih'inoo*. Could be." Grandfather took another sip of coffee and tossed the stone to me.

"So, the bright light I saw was a meteor shower?" I asked, as I caught the stone with my left hand.

"We could say that," Grandfather said.

"What about y'all's bull?" Jones asked. "Ain't no meteorite done nothing like that before."

"What exactly did happen to your bull, Grandfather," JEEP asked.

"Yeah, tell us. But, start from when y'all left us at Blue's yesterday," Jones added.

They sat and listened to us tell of the events of the afternoon. I described the lights as I remember seeing them, and finding the bull. Grandfather described the bull's injuries in great detail to JEEP, who kept asking specific questions to both of us.

Then, JEEP jumped up and ran to the door. He grabbed his book bag and coat and stopped long enough to mumble about remembering something and he'd call later. He was gone with the slamming of the door.

"Wonder what got his slacks in a bundle.

He pops in and out like a squirrel in a nut factory," Jones said.

"Yeah, kind of annoying," I said.

"I'm getting used to it," Blue said, then added, "makes me feel young."

"Hmphf!" was all Grandfather said to that.

* * *

"*Nebesiibehe*? Do you believe it was a meteor shower I saw?" I picked up my dinner plate and took it to the sink.

The rest of the gang had left hours ago.

"I couldn't say, *Hono'ie Neeceeebi*. But, if I recall, the skies were awful cloudy. Don't know if one could see the stars fall on an afternoon like that." Grandfather washed my plate and handed it back to me.

"So, I'm not crazy, but it wasn't a meteoroid?"

"We could say it was."

"But you don't really believe it was, do you, *Nebesiibehe*?" I asked, as I dried the dishes.

"I believe what you saw and what I saw many years ago was the same. I believe no stone butchered our bull. But, other than that, I cannot say."

"*Hohóu, Nebesiibehe.*"

"You are very welcome, *Hono'ie Neeceeebi*. Don't always believe your eyes, but don't always doubt them, either. Sometimes an egg is just an egg, but sometimes it's a chicken."

The phone rang, and at the same time, someone knocked on our front door.

I looked at Grandfather.

He looked at me.

The phone rang again.

The knocking became harder.

"You get the phone, *Hono'ie Neeceeebi*. I'll see who's at the door."

* * *

"Greetings, Buck," JEEP's voice came from the other end of the phone. "I just got finished with my extensive research. First, please let me apologize for running out on you fellas so quickly. But, I have some interesting points to consider about your bull and I think I've figured it out. It seems all animal mutilations reported in the past 30 years..."

"Hold on a second, JEEP, Grandfather's trying to tell me something." I put the phone receiver to my chest, and turned to Grandfather. "Yes, *Nebesiibehe*, did you need something?"

"I'm sorry, *Hono'ie Neeceeebi*. I've let you down. They've come to take you. Hang up the phone and come with me."

"Come on, son. Time to go." Deputy Blankenship pushed past Grandfather, almost knocking him down and grabbed my arm hard.

I dropped the receiver, and felt myself being pulled in my bare feet and without a coat through the snow. The world spun around and my head felt light.

"*Nebesiibehe?* What's going on?" I asked, but I couldn't find Grandfather anywhere. Deputy Blankenship yanked my arms behind me and I felt ice-cold metal clamp down hard around my wrists.

"This can't be happening," I thought to myself.

Visions of my parents being handled this way not too long ago entered my head. My eyes burned and my throat welled. Deputy

Blankenship shoved me onto the back of his car and slammed the door shut, almost catching my foot.

The back seat of the deputy's cruiser was enclosed in a cage. I could see a big, black rifle attached to the dash of the car. There was also a monitor with a small keyboard and a mike on a curly wire. I felt sick to my stomach and I wasn't able to stop shaking.

Then, I remembered seeing on a reality TV show there's a camera and microphone inside a cop's car, so I figured Deputy Blankenship couldn't harm me... too much, anyway.

I watched as he got in behind the wheel. The car dipped down from his weight. He let out a loud fart, slammed his door, and started the engine.

"Travis basically tells me you actually beat him up this morning. Is that right, boy?"

"No, Sir. I didn't."

"Don't lie to me, now, boy. My kid wouldn't be making this stuff up."

"Is that why I'm under arrest?"

"You ain't literally under arrest. Don't wet your little girl panties. Basically, we just need to take you down to the station and give you some actual talking to."

Deputy Blankenship pulled out of Grandfather's drive and headed south toward town. A horrible smell hit my nose and made me gag. It reminded me of the Easter egg I found last August by stepping on it. Stunk up the whole dang house for weeks.

I tried to put my face into my chest to get some fresh air, but couldn't move well with my hands cuffed behind me. I took a deep breath through my mouth and turned my head as far to the right as I could.

I scooted over to the other side of the car so I wasn't sitting directly behind Deputy

Blankenship, but nothing helped much.

Just when I thought I'd be able to breathe again, he let another one rip through the car. It smelled worse than the first one.

The car came to a sudden stop. I lurched forward. My head hit the caged wall behind the front passenger seat. The world started to swim again and everything went black around me. I felt my body being pulled from the car and half-dragged through the snow and into the brightly-lit sheriff's office.

"Bring him in here, Tom," a voice said from somewhere.

My head started to clear as I entered a small room with a square table and three chairs. Only one was empty.

"Actually, I was just gonna..." Deputy Blankenship stopped talking at the sight of JEEP and a well-dressed man seated in two of the chairs.

"That's far enough," the man said, standing up. He took me from the deputy's grasp and steadied me. "Take off those cuffs," he said to Deputy Blankenship.

Then, turning to the Sheriff, he added, "Why is this boy cuffed?" The well-dressed man then pointed to my aching forehead. "Did your man do this to him?"

"No, Sir. I literally did not touch the actual suspect other than to basically subdue him with the handcuffs, Sir," Deputy Blankenship said, as he removed the cuffs.

"Did he do this to you?" the man asked me.

"No, Sir. I hit my head on the cage when he stopped." I rubbed my wrists.

It felt good to get the cuffs off. It felt even better to breathe fresh, clean air.

I touched my forehead and winced from the pain it caused.

Then, I realized JEEP was in the room.

Why is JEEP here?

I looked at him and raised my right eyebrow. This week was getting stranger by the minute.

"Allow me to introduce my father," JEEP said, and then added, "your attorney, Mr. Eugene Parker."

❧ Chapter Eight ❧

Nun-The-Less

"Gonza, Buck! What happened next?"

Blue sat on the buffalo rug in the greatroom, holding a cup of cocoa in her hands. The gang came over right after school. Grandfather said I didn't have to go to school, what with the arrest and all.

"Well, Mr. Parker said they didn't have anything to hold me on, and since the bull was killed on private property, and Grandfather wasn't about to press charges, he said they had no other option than to let me go home. And, about that time Grandfather showed up with my coat and shoes, so I went home."

"Do they still think you, like, killed your grandfather's bull, and drank its blood?"

"Are y'all fixin to sue? Yer head looks like a pancake assaulted by a waffle iron," Jones said.

"Yeah, they think I killed the bull in the Northern Arapaho Hill of Life Ritual and no, we won't sue," I said. "I'm just glad it's over."

"Well, actually, nothing is over," JEEP said. "We still have to ascertain how the bull ended up like that and what those lights were in the sky right before. And, that's why I called you last night. To relay what I learned on the Internet about your grandfather's bull.

"I looked up cattle mutilations and found the same exact markers indicated on all strange occurrences in this area, and others. It seems to me there are no scientific explanations regarding these mutilations, and therefore the only intelligent, plausible explanation might be extraterrestrial in nature."

"What did you just say?" Blue asked.

"Yeah, come again..." Jones said.

"ETs. The only explanation is an alien life form – the crop circle, the flashes of lights and the bull," JEEP said.

"I thought you didn't believe in science fiction mumbo-jumbo," I said.

"Well, as in Ockham's Razor... you know?" JEEP looked around at all of us, one at a time. "No?"

I had no idea what Ockham's Razor was, so I just shrugged when he looked my way.

"The simplest explanation or strategy tends to be the best one. When all other possible avenues have been thoroughly explored, what other explanation do we have? Other than a misguided satanic ritual and I gotta tell you fellas, I'd rather believe in aliens," JEEP said.

"Gonza, people, we better get moving. We have to get ready for treating. Meet back here in, like, two hours?" Blue asked.

"Have you decided what you're going to be?" I asked.

"Yes, and it's a surprise," she said.

"Me, too," said JEEP.

* * *

I put on my nun costume and walked into the greatroom where Grandfather sat by the fire.

"How do I look?" I asked him.

"Oooo, scary, *Hono'ie Neeceeebi.* Just like I remembered," he said.

"Oh, wait a second. I have something to complete the outfit." Grandfather got up and walked out of the room. He came back in with an old, wooden ruler in his hand.

"Here," he said, handing it to me.

"What's this for?"

"To keep your friends in line. One whack across the knuckles ought to do it." Grandfather chuckled and sat back down on the rug.

I turned the ruler over in my hand. It looked really old.

"Where did you get this?"

"Took it from an ugly nun. Thought you might want it back." He chuckled some more.

"There's a bag for your candy by the door. Did you put your long johns on under the habit?" Grandfather asked.

"Yes, *Nebesiibehe*."

"Okay. I'll meet you at *Sitee Hiitonih-'inoo*'s later."

A knock on the door beckoned me and I opened it to see a scarecrow, a skeleton, and a short pumpkin.

"I thought you were going to be Dorothy," I said to the scarecrow.

"Are you the kid that killed that bull and drank his blood?" the skeleton asked, and I realized they weren't my friends at all.

"*Nebesiibehe*, could you get this?" I called to Grandfather.

When he came to the door, I whispered in his ear, "I'm going out the back way. If the guys come up, tell them to meet me at the trough."

* * *

"Hey, Buck!"

"Yeah?" I answered. "Where are you guys?"

"Coming, just," Blue said.

Out of the darkening light, I saw Dorothy carrying a stuffed dog in a basket, walking with a silver alien robot.

"Cool costume, Blue," I said.

"Thanks, me mum made it. She was inspired by the past few days. Me mum loves aliens and UFOs."

"She sewed my costume, too," Jones said. "Y'all ain't never seen a better Dorothy, I'd bet."

"And, your costume is smashing," Blue said to me.

"What about mine?" JEEP's voice coming out of nowhere made me jump a little.

"What the... Where did you come from?" I asked.

"Don't end your sentence in a preposition or I'll smack you with my ruler," JEEP said, as he came into view.

Standing before us was a smaller version of me, ruler and all.

"Just call me Nun-the-Less," he said.

* * *

"Well, that was extremely fun and lucrative," JEEP said, carrying his large bag of candy. We were headed back to Blue's house after going door-to-door.

"I'm thinking ya better hand it all over right now," a voice came from the dormant honeysuckle bushes as we passed. Travis stepped out from behind them and grabbed a handful of Dorothy's braids.

"Ow!" Jones screamed.

"Travis, don't make me remind you what I've mastered in my young life," JEEP said.

Two shadows appeared from behind us, and grabbed JEEP. Travis' posse had JEEP pinned to the ground before we knew what was happening.

"Them nun dresses make it hard to run, don't it?" Travis laughed, but it wasn't a happy sound. I felt a shiver run down my spine. He yanked at Jones' hair again. She screamed in pain and fear. Blue took a step closer to me and grabbed my hand. I squeezed hers for comfort, but I don't know if I was comforting her, or me.

"Give 'em over, or Dorothy loses a braid or two."

"Sure, Travis. Whatever you say. Come

on, you guys, do what he says." I dropped my bag in the snow at my feet. Blue and Jones dropped theirs, too. One of the kids holding JEEP took his bag, and ran to Travis.

"Git them other bags, too," Travis said. The boys did as they were told.

"Well, thank you very much for your help in gathering all this candy. You'll be glad to know it won't go to any waste, except mine," he said, and then turned to Jones, "I oughta pull one out just for what Runtface did to me yesterday." He pulled harder on her hair, causing her to scream.

I stepped up to Travis and grabbed the hand holding her braids, stopping the pulling.

"Let go of her. You got our candy. Just go and leave us alone." I hoped he couldn't feel my hand shaking. Jones was crying.

JEEP walked up and put his hands out in front of him, like they show in the kung-futype movies on TV. If I hadn't been so scared, I probably would've laughed.

"Do you require a reminder, now that your goons have released me?"

Travis let go of Jones' braids. "You tell anyone it was you and not Chief what beat me up, and I'll kill you dead, you hear?" He turned to his friends who held the bags of candy. "Forgit you heard that. Let's go."

The sky lit up with a bright white streak of light above us, making Travis and his friends stop in their tracks. We all looked up to see a bright red-orange ball hovering above our heads. A loud, humming sound grew in my ears and I clamped my hands over them. I noticed the others did the same. A beam of reddish-orange light beamed down on us, like a search light, bathing each one of us in bright light, one at a time.

Travis' body rose from the ground. He let

out a scream louder and shriller than Jones ever could. He floated for about a foot, then dropped with a thud into the snow below. The snow poofed up around him, like it did with Grandfather's bull. Travis curled up in the snow and cried. The skies darkened again, and the light-ball disappeared in mid-air.

"Is that what you saw, Buck?" JEEP whispered, staring at the empty sky.

"Yeah, that or something like it."

"Gonza, Buck. What do you think it was?"

"The same thing you guys think it was," I said.

Jones didn't say anything. She sniffled loudly and rubbed her sore head, with her eyes fixed on Travis.

I looked at Travis lying in the snow. I could see snow melting beneath him.

"I surmise he urinated in his trousers," JEEP said.

Travis got up and looked at us with crazy eyes, then at the sky and at his friends. He was about to say something when his jaw dropped open, revealing a ghastly, gaping hole. He let out a blood-curdling scream; fear tore through his eyes. He took off running in the other direction. His friends ran after him, abandoning our bags of candy in the snow.

I turned to see what it was that frightened Travis so badly. Walking through the field was an elongated shape. It had a large head with dark, almond-shaped eyes and a green glow. It trudged through the snow toward us.

I almost screamed, myself. Then, I noticed the moccasins poking out from beneath the alien costume.

"*Nebesiibehe?*" I asked.

"*Hebe, Hono'ie Neeceeebi.* Fancy meeting you here."

* * *

"Well, that was an exciting adventure. Do you fellas always have this much fun?" JEEP asked, as we sat around Blue's kitchen table examining our candy for bad pieces.

Mrs. B had placed a large bowl in the center for us to throw the half-opened or questionable candy.

"Yep. When we can," Jones said. "Hey, thanks for coming to my rescue back there."

"Where do you suppose aliens fit in to religion, reincarnation, and myth?" Blue asked, and stuck a green sucker into her mouth.

"Momma says ain't no such thing as aliens. She says the devil is in charge of everything but the earth," Jones said, and tossed an unwrapped bubblegum into the bowl.

"Do you believe her?" Blue asked.

Jones shrugged.

"Grandfather says we all are one; aliens, you guys, me, angels. He says there's no beginning and no end, just the here and the now."

"That's right, *Hono'ie Neeceeebi*," Grandfather shouted from the living room. "That boy learns well," I heard him say to Mrs. B.

"Well, father says we are born and we die and that's all there is," JEEP said. "And, what we make of our life in the interim is neither here nor there, because it doesn't really matter in the end. Just be happy, and be the best you can possibly be. When you're gone, you'll live on through the memories of the people you left behind who love you." JEEP handed a Bit-O-Honey to me. "These things make me vomit," he added.

"What do you think, Blue?" I asked.

"I don't rightly know, you know? I know what I saw tonight wasn't, like, anything I've ever seen before. I know what I think it might bloody well be, but I won't be telling anyone about it. I want to believe what me dad said about living on through love and such, but seeing is believing."

"Well, maybe... and then again, maybe not. You guys saw that thing in the sky, but you don't want to believe it. Maybe we have it backwards. Maybe believing is seeing. Maybe we are the masters of our own destiny, but only our own destiny, and at the end of our lives, what we believe to be the truth becomes true for us. I mean, maybe Jones ends up in heaven, because that's what she believes, but I'll be reincarnated. Maybe having something to believe in truly is what gets us through another day," I said.

"And another adventure," Jones added.

"Here's to another adventure." JEEP said, as he picked up his glass of punch and toasted.

* 〰 👽 〰 *

The Elementary Adventures of Jones, JEEP, Buck & Blue

Complete Edition

JEEP
book 4

Sandra Miller Linhart

To all the children who follow their heart regardless of how many obstacles well-meaning people place in their path.

Life *is* but a dream, so row merrily.

(...but keep your oars in your own boat.)

"Thank you" to my first reader and personal hero – my big sister, Donda, for keeping me on track, in line and up to par. And, she knew how to spell 'nigh on' when I didn't. Bonus!

"Thank yous" to my 12-year-old advisor and niece, Heather Louise Stettler, for her complete description of inedible school lunches, notable discussions and what is and is not 'cool' in 6th grade... and to my own Uncle Ivan, who sparked my imagination with his colorful tales of the old goldmine he found once upon a time in these here hills of Colorado.

Sandra

Table of Contents

୫ $ ଔ

❥ Chapter One ❧

A Friend In Need

"Do you really think he found gold?" Meaghan questioned our great-uncle Ivan.

A few of my siblings and I assembled... means gathered... around him at the dining room table. His old, rough hands held a full, tepid... uh, lukewarm... cup of black coffee.

The aroma filled my nostrils with a hearty bouquet. I knew from personal experience, however, coffee often smelled superior to its flavor.

Uncle Ivan hadn't had the opportunity to taste it yet. He'd been imparting yet another of his rich stories.

This particular one was quite intriguing... interesting.

"Yeah, is there really gold in them there hills?" Maxwell inquired.

Maxwell's my amusing brother, whereas Meaghan's my gullible sister. Separated in age by only eight months, they appear to be twins. Currently, they're both 14 – six years my senior. In a few weeks, Max will turn 15.

"Yep, Max, I do believe there is and, Meggie girl, I do believe he did." Ivan took a gulp of his lukewarm coffee and grimaced.

"Hey, Meg. Do ya think you could nuke this for your ol' uncle?" He offered his cup to Meaghan, who obediently jumped up.

Ivan had come over to spend his Sunday with us. He's the uncle of Diane, my mother. He doesn't call on us often. It's always interesting when he does.

"OK, but don't say anything good while I'm gone," Meg implored, as she took the cup from Uncle Ivan's outstretched hands.

"Where did you say the old man's cabin was?" Jax inquired.

Jackson's 18, and he's my preferred brother of the six I have, by far. He's an apprentice at Eugene's law firm. I believe he'd make a far better investigator than an attorney.

"On the left, as you're headed up Sink's Canyon Road. Just past Walt Shanahan's place. Immediately before the rise of the *Popo Agie* River. Anymore, I don't think much is left of it. But, when I was a boy it was something, all right."

"So, where was the mine?" Donald asked.

"And, how do we get there?" Ronald added.

Ronald and Donald are 16 and mono-zygotic twins... they came from the same egg... maternal twins, you know? They look identical. However, Don's a brain, like me, and Ron's a brawn.

"How much gold did he get?" Meaghan returned with Ivan's coffee. She held the apparently hot cup gingerly in her petite hands.

"And, I thought I said to not say anything good while I was gone."

"I'm not sure, but he was pretty excited. Seems his grandfather staked the claim as a younger man. Then, when the old man's father mined it, the cavern flooded.

"The rising water cut off access to any gold. The old man figured out how to rig up a pump to siphon the water. Only then could he get to the large vein his father discovered."

"Do you suppose he succeeded?" I positioned my chair nearer Ivan's.

"Well, I don't rightly know. The last time I was up there, oh, I'd say nigh on 50 years ago, the rigging was there. Water ran from the piping in a pretty steady stream.

"So, yeah, I guess maybe he did. But, at that time there weren't nary much left of the front of the old cabin. Just some timber and tin. And, there's an old outhouse in back. Anymore, I'd bet one could find it easily enough."

The phone rang, and although I hate to admit it, it made me jump a tad.

Meaghan scurried to answer it. She always did. For some reason it seems girls and phones aren't separated for long.

"James, phone's for you," she called from the kitchen.

* * *

"Your folks are rich, right?" Blue's voice sounded hesitant over the wire.

"Um, I'm unaware of their financial status. One could assume so. Eugene's an attorney and Diane's a pharmacist. However, one item seldom brought to my attention are the monetary matters of this household. Why do you inquire? Oh, you're contemplating Jones' 12th birthday! What is it you desire to purchase for her?"

"Gonza, no! Give us a break, JEEP! Not her birthday. This is ways more important than a bloody anniversary," Blue replied.

"Whatever could be more important than a birthday?"

I, for one, never neglect the opportunity to celebrate my existence with flare on the anniversary of my birth. I tried to instill the same reverence in everyone surrounding me.

"Your curt reply is somewhat distressing to me, Blue."

"She'd bloody kill me if she knew I was talking to you about this," Blue started, and then stopped.

I waited a tad for her to continue.

The silence kept interrupting.

"The question I pose to you now is: *'What is up, Blue?'*"

"Gonza! Me mum's already home from picking up Jones from church! I have to go. They'll be coming up the stairs any minute now. Don't dare say anything to her about this!"

The steady buzzing in my ear indicated Blue had truncated the call. She left me hanging on the line like, as Jones would say, last week's wash.

I returned to the dining room just in time to see our little group dispersing. Ivan continued to sit with a cup in his hands. Upon approach, I observed his cup was empty.

"If I refill your cup might you divulge more about that cabin and goldmine?" I inquired.

"I sure will, Little Man." He held out his cup.

* * *

Buck stood outside the school's east side. He rubbed his hands together, while he waited for the morning bell to chime.

I approached him from behind.

"Did Blue converse with you yesterday?"

Buck jumped a tad at my voice.

"Crikey, JEEP! Why do you always do that? Sneaking up on a guy like that. Yes ... and no. Not really."

"What is all this about Jones?"

"I don't know, but it's annoying. I wish Blue'd just come out and say what the deal is." Buck shoved his hands deep into his pockets.

"I understand your distress. She communicated somewhat in riddles, inquiring as to the income of Eugene and Diane. For some mysterious reason."

"Who are Eugene and Diane?" Buck inquired.

"My parents."

"Why on earth do you call them by their first names?"

"Well, for no other reason than those are their names. They don't call me offspring, or child, you know. They, unlike you fellas, call me James. Or, James Edward Eugene Parker. Or, a variation thereof. However do you label your parents?"

"I call my father *Neisonoo*, and my mother *Neinoo* – the *Inuna-Ina* words for father and mother. Their real names are Robert, like me, and Mary Black. And, as you know, I call Grandfather *Nebesiibehe*."

"How are your parents, anyway?" I inquired.

I felt a little peculiar bringing up such a tender topic with Buck.

"Good, I guess. Grandfather says they might get visitation rights soon. They may want to see me. I guess families get to talk with the rehab counselors to work out issues, or something like that."

"Do you desire to meet with them - your parents?"

"Um, yeah. I suppose. I'm not afraid of getting hurt anymore. I think. Anyway, I guess I'll cross that bridge when I get to it."

Buck buried his neck in the collar of his coat. He stomped up and down in the snow.

The morning bell chimed. We pivoted to get in line.

The rushing assembly of kids walked up the stairs through the immense wooden doors.

"I deduce the girls yearn to be tardy today," I stated.

"I suppose," Buck replied.

* * *

"So, what's the story?" Buck inquired, as Blue walked up to our lunch table.

She carried a lunch tray.

"Where's Jones?" I inquired.

"She received some, like, bad news yesterday and won't be coming to school today. Maybe not tomorrow, either."

Blue positioned her tray opposite Buck. She sat alongside me, as customary.

"Is that the reasoning behind your mysterious phone call?" I inquired.

I pulled the bag of cheese puffs from my lunch sack and opened it.

A poof of cheesy, orange dust satisfactorily swam in the air toward my nostrils.

Their scent enticed my taste buds.

"Yes. I need some help. I don't know what to do. I promised Jones I wouldn't say a bloody word about this to anyone. Not even you two blokes. But, gonza! She's me friend, you know? I feel as if I have to do something."

"Mum's the word. You have my word on it," I reassured her, with cheesy breath.

I extended an orange-stained hand to seal the deal. Blue just looked at it.

She turned to Buck.

I retrieved my hand. I dug into the bag for another puff of cheese.

"You know her dad's been in rehab since he got injured in war?" she started.

"Yeah, I remember. The roadside bomb – IED, or something like that took his right forearm. It messed up his legs pretty bad too, right?" Buck inquired.

"He's being taught to walk again at Walter Reed Medical Center, correct?" I added.

"Yes, you're both right. Anyway, we got a call yesterday from Mrs. J as Jones was getting ready for church..."

Blue took a deep breath and continued. "Promise you won't, like, tell a soul what I'm about to tell you."

"Promise," Buck and I responded, simultaneously.

Blue took another deep breath.

"Mr. J had what Mrs. J called a set-back. I guess he has some shrapnel... pieces of the bomb imbedded in his left leg. The docs missed it at first. Now he's got an infection from it. Mrs. J said the docs think he might lose his leg." Blue picked at her mashed potatoes with her fork.

"Man, that's just awful," Buck responded.

I didn't know what to say.

"That's not the worst of it either," Blue replied. Tears trickled down her face.

"They said if they can't get his fever down and he doesn't start fighting the bloody infection... he'll die."

❧ Chapter Two ❧

ASK, AND IT IS GIVEN

"So, you require money to purchase, what? Superior doctors? Enhanced care?" My cheese puffs no longer tempted me.

I placed the bag on the table. I wiped my hands on my trousers.

The action left two orange tracks across the fabric on my legs.

Diane's gonna annihilate me for that.

"No. I want to send Jones to Washington, DC to see her father before he dies, or whatnot."

"Crikey! Do you really think he's gonna die?"

"Just how much currency are we discussing?" I inquired, forgetting about my streaked trousers and returned to the conversation at hand.

"I don't know. I haven't thought that far ahead. I just know I wish I'd seen me dad at least one more time before he was killed by that homicide bomber. If I could give anything to Jones it would be a ticket to be with her parents." Blue touched her red Phoenix feather.

It continually hung around her neck attached to Grandfather's medicine bag. She sniffed loudly and added, "For maybe the last time."

"When's her birthday?" Buck inquired.

"The 24th of November," I replied. "I suppose we could all combine our wealth and purchase an airline ticket."

"I have only $20.00 from my last birthday. I spent the rest on my Halloween costume," Buck stated.

"I have $115.86 at last count." I repositioned my spectacles. I swept the hair from my eyes.

"Me mum borrowed all me savings for me little brother, Prince Charles' doctor bill. She says she'll pay me back when she can. Who knows when that'll be?"

"I'm no genius... well, yes, I suppose I am. However, I don't believe $135.86 will fly Jones very far."

* * *

"Diane, how expensive is it to catch a flight to Washington DC from here?"

"James, why are you calling me at work? Is this really important?"

"Well, yes, actually. We want to send Jones to see her parents. For, um, her birthday. I mean, Thanksgiving. Both, really."

"Very thoughtful. But, can't you figure that out by yourself?" My mother sounded rushed. "Gotta go. ...Oh! Just remember, it'll be more than just the cost of a plane ticket."

"What are you implying, Diane?"

"James, please!" Diane sighed loudly. "OK. Um, flight, food, lodging, you name it," she stated. Then she added, "I need to get back to work now, James."

"Wait, Diane. Could you and Eugene..."

"Oh, James, you know we're in no financial position. Harrison, Sharin and Darin are all in college. Jackson soon will follow. But, if you need any other kind of help, you know we're there for you. Gotta go, sweetie. See you at home in a bit." And with that, Diane disconnected.

Diane was correct. *Just how much are we discussing?* I collected a quantity of paper and commenced brainstorming.

If Jones boards a flight from here... Wait, are there any flights from here? I knew Lander had a modest airport. I didn't remember seeing any commercial flights arriving or departing. Just bi-planes and Cessnas and the like. *So, where is the nearest, considerable airport? Riverton? Casper? Cheyenne? And, how will we transport her?* I wrote, '1: Transportation to airport' on the paper.

Once she arrives at the airport, what will be the duration of her flight? Might she endure any layovers? And if so, for how long?

I wrote on the page, '2: Flight time, number of layovers, 3: Meals needed during flight, 4: Average cost of meals.'

Now, how might she get from the airport to the clinic?

'5: Mileage from airport to clinic, 6: Average cost of taxis in Washington DC,' I added to my list.

When she arrives at the clinic, she can lodge with her mom. Presumably, her parents will feed her while there. I made one more addendum to my list: '7: Spending money.'

Wow. That's plenty to consider. I repositioned my spectacles and brushed my hair from my eyes. *I need to ask Diane to clip my bangs.*

I launched my search engine and googled airfare from Lander, WY to Washington DC. It came back: 'Error. No airport found.'

I searched the list. Casper. Jackson Hole. Cheyenne. I typed in Casper, and hit enter.

It's approximately two hours from Lander, a bit closer than the other cities. It again came back: 'Error. At least one adult must travel with a child.' I indicated one adult, no child.

It'll give us an approximate figure from which to start. Children fly alone every day.

I hit enter again. This time I got results. I printed out my searches and continued on. *I'll have to figure it all out after I compile all available data.*

Next on my list... *Hmmm, numbers 2-4 may be worked out from the printed data. Mileage from airport to clinic...*

I typed mapquest.com into my browser. I input Dulles International Airport and Walter Reed Medical Center. *About thirty miles between the two. 30.84, to be exact. Hmmm.*

"James! Dinner's ready. Get the lead out!" Max's voice bellowed in the hall, making me start a bit.

I looked around my darkening room.

The screen-saver star field displayed on my monitor indicated I must have drifted off.

The pool of saliva on my paper affirmed my assumptions to be correct.

My head felt fuzzy.

My saliva smeared the last thought I'd written. I wiped the spit away, and tried to decipher the smear.

'ASK, AND IT IS GIVEN,' was written in bold letters in the middle of the paper.

Just prior to those words, I'd written, 'I need to find the address of the Airport to run a taxi calculator to figure the cost of said taxi.'

I moved my computer mouse.

The star field disappeared.

It was replaced by the official taxi cab calculator of Washington DC. 'Dulles International Airport' had been typed in the point of origin field. An error message indicated the physical address required input.

"When did I do that?" I wondered aloud.

"JAMES! I said get the lead out. Mom's waiting dinner on you, for pity sake! And, I'm starving." I heard Max's voice fade as he descended the stairwell, headed presumably toward the dining room.

ASK, AND IT IS GIVEN

What a peculiar thing to have written. And, in bold, no less. Huh!

I left my room with the phrase replaying itself in my mind. *How very peculiar.*

ASK, AND IT IS GIVEN

The evening meal menu wafted to me via my nostrils as I descended the stairs. The aroma announced buttery, mashed potatoes and some kind of spicy, cooked beef.

I'll evade the beef, if I can get away with it. However, I'd eat the potatoes.

If they aren't at all lumpy, of course.

I hoped Diane prepared dinner rolls.

❦ Chapter Three ❧

NOT AS IT SEEMS

"Does the phrase 'Ask, and it is given' mean anything to you fellas?" I inquired at lunch the next day.

Lunch was becoming our main meeting place; our round table for the Knights of Adventure, it seemed.

"Sure," Jones responded, with a mouth full of broccoli. It was her favorite vegetable since Blue accurately convinced her it contained more calcium than milk. And, unlike milk's calcium, the stuff in broccoli is easily digested. Also, Jones despised milk. It all worked out for the betterment.

"Sure," she repeated. "It's in the Bible. Gimmee a sec." Jones face screwed up into concentration central. Our surrounding area became tranquil. The voices and sounds from the other students in the lunchroom echoed around our thought bubble like spirits from another realm.

I quietly popped a cheese puff into my mouth. I pushed my spectacles up in anticipation of her answer. The question had plagued my dreams all night.

"Um, the Gospel according to St. Matthew, chapter seven, verse seven. 'Ask, and it shall be given you: Seek, and ye shall find: Knock and it shall be opened unto you.

"Then, it goes on to say: For every one that asketh receiveth; and he that seeketh findeth; and to him that knocketh it shall be opened.'"

Jones opened her eyes. She took another bite of broccoli. She then added with a full mouth, "It's also quoted in St. Luke, chapter eleven, verse nine."

"Wow, that's redundant!" I stated.

"Crikey, no! That's amazing!" Buck's eyes were wide.

"That was 'tastic, Jones... how come you can remember all that? You can't hardly remember when Columbus sailed the ocean blue."

"1942, right?" Jones flashed a huge broccoli grin.

"No, 1942!? Crikey, Jones! We were right in the middle of World War II in 1942. The United States had just help to create the United Nations," Buck replied.

"By then, of course we'd already been 'discovered by Columbus' – what a farce that was. Discovered! Crikey! Discovered that the area had already been discovered by my ancestors, you mean." Buck mumbled, and shook his head in disgust.

"1492, Jones. 1492! How complicated is

that after the tome you just quoted?" I laughed.

"Why d'ya need to know, anyways? I ain't thinkin' y'all are supposed to be talkin' about the bible and bible stuff in class." Jones stopped chewing. "Separation, and all that." Her eyes bore into mine. She waited for my answer.

"Um..." *I can't tell her what I'm doing.* I wasn't supposed to know about her father.

"Um..." I repeated.

"Gonza, JEEP! You're a great orator... means speaker," Blue stated.

The trio burst into laughter. I felt no contempt from her words. I smiled, and pushed my spectacles up my nose.

"Well, to be totally candid, I kind of, well, dreamt it last night. I was unaware from whence it came." I couldn't stop smiling.

Blue's giggling continued.

"Me mum's reading a book with, like, the same title. I don't think it's about the Bible, though. Knowing me mum, it's a right cry from it." Blue wiped the laughter tears from her eyes. "I could ask her what it's about."

"Would you, please? And, Buck, could you inquire to Grandfather if it means any- thing to him, as well?"

"Sure, but I think it's pretty clear. If you ask for it, you'll get it. And, since you asked me, you'll get it. No need to thank me. I know I'm great." Buck did a little birthday dance in his seat, singing, "Yeah, I'm great. I'm great. I know, I know, I'm great."

"Grating on my nerves, you mean." Travis towered above us. He stood behind Buck and Jones. Travis' hands rested on his hips.

Buck immediately stopped his dance. He froze in his seat, as did Jones and Blue.

I let out an audible groan.

Blue kicked my leg under the table.

"Ouch! Travis, I think your alien acquaintances are calling you. Why don't you just go beam up somewhere else?" I inquired, and rubbed my shin.

"Listen here, little Runtface, Gruntface..."

He didn't complete his statement before Mr. Reed, our music teacher, and one of the men who pulled him from the grips of death just weeks before, walked up and put his arm around Travis' shoulders.

"Hey, there, Mr. Blankenship. Coming to thank your friends here for rescuing you?"

"Yassir."

"Good. Good thing. You know, you might have frozen to death if these kids hadn't found you," Mr. Reed continued.

The incident took place prior to meeting my friends. However, I had become aware of it in the interim.

Travis' face grew scarlet. I couldn't tell if it was infuriation or embarrassment that fed it, though. I pushed my spectacles up and listened.

"If I remember correctly, you stated they gave you some kind of meat."

"Dog meat," Jones whispered under her breath.

Travis stiffened and started toward her. Mr. Reed held him back with a gentle arm. We all looked straight ahead; statues in our seats. I had a peculiar feeling we would pay for this episode sometime later. I hoped it wouldn't be too terrible an experience.

"Mr. Blankenship. I see your leg wasn't broken after all."

"Nossir, just twisted a bit."

"So, they said. So, they said. Lucky, lucky you. OK, go ahead. Tell your friends how grateful you are."

Mr. Reed waited with his arm across Travis' shoulders. His hand clasped over Travis' arm and squeezed a bit.

"Ow! Um, yeah, thanks guys. I, uh, need to say thanks, I guess for, uh, finding me."

Mr. Reed dropped his arm to his side. He said, "There now, that's much better. You guys play nice." He backed away from us, saying to Travis, "Move along, now. You're done here."

"Don't think I've forgotten it's your fault I was in that there hole in the first place, punks," Travis growled under his breath.

He turned to leave. Then, he pointed directly at me, and added, "I still owe you one for that Halloween night trick, too, don't you forgit. I know I won't."

Travis turned his attention to Buck and said, "Just you remember, Chief. It's huntin' season. That makes you Sitting Duck."

Travis disappeared behind the lunchroom doors.

"Well, that boy makes about as much sense as a duck's toothbrush," Jones stated.

"Thank Buddha, he's gone," Blue stated. She sighed loudly in relief.

"Oh, he may be gone for now. I'm sure we haven't seen the last of him," Buck responded.

"Undeniably!" I added.

* * *

"Hey, Jax. Do you think there's anything to that goldmine anecdote Uncle Ivan told us?"

"No, James, I don't and I'll tell you why." Jackson sat next to me on the living room couch.

"During the gold rush of 1859, miners found gold in Colorado a plenty. But, even ten years later hardly any had been found in these mountains."

"That doesn't mean gold was not unearthed," I responded.

"True. I can't argue with that."

"What does 'ask, and it is given' mean to you?"

"I'm pretty sure it's a passage in the Bible. I read it to mean that whatever you ask of God, your prayers will be answered."

"Oh, is that it?" Even I could hear the disappointment in my own voice. *Why would I have written that? Pray to a God I believe has no logical basis in society except to control the masses? To keep order in an otherwise chaotic civilization? To give structure to a culture in order to preserve its existence? No, I don't think I would have written something from the Bible.*

"Why sound so disappointed, James? Not the answer you were looking for?"

"Not really. However, I don't know what I anticipated in your reply. So... if I requested money from you, would you grant it to me?"

"What for?"

"That, I cannot convey, Jax. You'll have to trust me when I state I truly need it."

"Depends. How much do you need?"

"As much as you can provide." I had calculated we needed a minimum of $850.00 for Jones' journey. It seemed like a massive amount of money.

"Here's $20." Jax placed a wadded-up bill in my hand. "That should be more than enough to get you whatever you could need."

"Thanks, Jax. I truly appreciate it."

"You're welcome, my man. Glad I could help." Jackson arose, and vacated the premises.

I sat alone in the vast living room. I contemplated the fireplace for awhile.

Maybe that was the message! Maybe I just needed to ask and people would present money! Soon we'd have sufficient funds for Jones.

I jumped up from the couch. I shoved the wadded bill into my pocket. I approached the phone. I looked up the number to the Valley Journal in the directory.

I dialed the number and waited.

"Valley Journal. How may I direct your call?"

"May I please have your email address for 'Letters to the Editor'?"

"Please hold," she replied.

I listened over the phone to the orchestra play Beethoven's *Ode to Joy* while I awaited her return.

The music stopped abruptly. Her voice replaced it. "Thank you for holding."

I wrote down the information she gave me.

I ran up to my room, and pulled up my email. I started writing a letter to the editor of our local newspaper:

To Whom It May Concern:

I am a young man whose class-mate is in dire need. I am there-fore requesting assistance from my community for this person. I'm unable to give any specifics, however, I would implore you look inside your hearts.

Please send any donation you feel appropriate to the Valley Journal, in care of The Little Man.
Thank you for your time,

'The Little Man'
James Edward Eugene Parker
(307) 555-4383

(Editor, please refrain from post-ing my name. I will be available to answer any questions through this email address, or telephon-ically after normal school hours. Thank you. JP)

I clicked 'send' and sighed. I felt assured

everything would work out for the best. I began to arise, and then returned to my seat.

I composed similar notes to my extended family members and family friends. However, I signed my real name. I made the request somewhat more personal. I omitted anything to do with the health and well-being of Jones' father or her dire situation. I, again, felt overly confident my plea would be fruitful.

ASK, AND IT IS GIVEN.

My task was complete: I asked.

Events would work out. I just knew it.

It couldn't help but be given.

✎ Chapter Four ✐

To Give or Forgive

"What are y'all having for Thanksgiving?" Jones inquired after a long silence in the lunchroom.

It was fish day.

Only I remembered to pack a lunch, as I do so daily.

The fellas sat looking dejectedly at their trays. They seemed to not want to touch even the coleslaw for fear the fish had contaminated it. And, none of the fellas wanted stomach cramps the rest of the day. I considered offering up my fare. I decided against it. No sense all of us departing the lunchroom famished.

"Turkey, potatoes, you know, the usual works," I replied.

"Crikey, I wish I had some of that right now," Buck interjected. "With corn on the cob and golden-browned *cebeteenocoo* or *nono'einoc*."

"Golden-browned what?" Blue inquired.

"Speaking of gold," I interrupted the chain-of-food-thought. "My Uncle Ivan visited Sunday last. He informed of us an old abandoned goldmine in the Sinks Canyon State Park. Pretty cool, if you fellas ask me."

I shoved a cheese puff into my mouth. I sucked it flat.

"Golden-browned frybread and flatbread. *Inuna-Ina* traditional breads. I'll make them for you guys someday."

Buck turned his attention from Blue to me. "Gold, huh? Do you believe him?"

"Have no reason to not. However, I'm

hesitant. Jax relates little gold was mined from the Wind River Mountain Range, if any, during the gold rushes in American history. Still, an enticing story, none-the-less."

"We usually eat, like, roasted goose with cranberry sauce and pumpkin pie for desert. Me mum never celebrated Thanksgiving until she married me dad, being an American tradition, and all. We're African-American, you know. But, me dad was from here. I think I overheard me mum saying we'd be eating at me Aunt Nan's house, or something."

"Dag-nabbit. I caught myself cravin' grits and sweet potatoes with pecan pie for dessert. I ain't knowin' if I'm gonna cotton to cooked goose." Jones' bottom lip began to tremble. Her sixteen, multi-colored banded braids bobbed as she lowered her head.

"I wonder what Mamma'd be having in Virginia. I'm feeling as out-of-place as a zipper on a diaper right about now," Jones said.

Blue and Buck looked at each other, and then me. I saw tears forming in Blue's eyes. I watched her touch her feather.

"Gonza, Jones, I don't know where we'll end up on Thanksgiving. I'm sure me mum will cook one of those things for you. Even if we do go to me Aunt Nan's."

"It don't matter none much." Jones stood. She picked up her tray. "Anyways, I gotta pee."

Jones dumped her uneaten food into the trash receptacle. She deposited her tray and hurried out of the lunchroom.

"Gonza, I wish we could really help her." Blue's eyes were still moist with tears.

"I estimate we need $850.00 for her entire trip. More would be optimum. We're now up to approximately $155.00, as my brother pitched in a twenty. I have an idea in the works to make more. What have you fellas in mind?"

"Bake sale? Car wash?"

"Crikey, Blue!" Buck said. "You're not in Georgia anymore! How in the world can we have a carwash smack-dab in Wyoming in the middle of winter?"

"Sorry, kind of forgot that bit. But, what about a bake sale? Me mum makes the biggest, 'tastic cookies in the known Universe. Why in Buddha's name can't we sell them for a dollar apiece?"

"You may inquire it of her. We can purchase ingredients with our existing funds." I pushed my spectacles up my nose. I sat on my legs on the bench. "So, here's the deal. Blue, you converse with your mother about baking the cookies. Buck, you talk to Grandfather about making those frybread thingies. I'll think of something, too. Call or email me this afternoon with a list of ingredients. I'll have my brother, Jax take me to the store. Agreed?"

"Agreed," they responded in unison.

"Agreed about what?" Jones inquired, as she sat back down. I hadn't noticed her walk up.

"Desserts for Thanksgiving," Buck quickly interjected. "What will you be wanting?"

"I dunno. What did y'all say?"

"I'm going to have me mum bake her gianormous cookies."

"I'm asking Grandfather for frybread."

"And, I'm requesting my favorite, Double-dark-chocolate brownies, no nuts. My oldest brother, Harrison, makes them best. So, Jones, what'll it be?"

"My mamma's sweet potato pie makes y'alls mouth wish it ain't never eaten anything else. Y'alls stomach'll agree. Maybe I can email Momma in a bit for the recipe." Her eyes were still muddled. However, the conversation seemed to brighten her spirits a tad.

"Maybe we all can celebrate Thanksgiving together," Jones said

"I know I'd much rather be with me friends than at me Aunt Nan's. Her bloody cats stink," said Blue.

"Just how many cats she gots I ain't knowin'. But, I spied seven just the other day. She's fixin' to have more cats than she gots marbles in her head."

* * *

"Thanks for assisting me with this, Jax. I fully appreciate it."

We lugged the groceries in and placed them on the kitchen counter. It progressively grew a bit nippy and dark outside.

"Sure thing, Little Man. You know I'd do anything for you. All you have to do is ask."

We deposited the perishables in the garage fridge, with a note to not touch. We kept the rest of our purchased ingredients in the grocery bags.

We would deliver it all to Blue's house when the coast was clear. Mrs. B acquiesced to do all the cooking, including the frybread. Grandfather intended to teach her the *Inuna-Ina* skill.

"What are you doing with all this food, anyway?"

"Kind of a school project... for Thanksgiving."

I despised falsifying my statements to Jax. However, I knew he'd understand my need for secrecy. It really wasn't that untrue. We *were* discussing capitalism in Social Studies.

"Speaking of school projects, I have homework. Thanks again, Jax."

I bolted upstairs to examine my email messages.

A response from the Valley Journal awaited me. I opened it with anticipation.

However, I reclined dejectedly back in my chair when I read:

Dear James,

I received your email asking for donations today. I wanted to let you know that I'm not comfortable printing it. Unfortunately, without knowing you or your character, I hesitate to print something asking my readers for money. I think my readers will be unable to gauge without more information about the specifics of your request whether they would be willing to send money. I think they'd be a lot more likely to give money to a young family member or close neighbor than you through your email. Therefore, your letter will not appear in the Valley Journal.

Thanks,
Al Graffiti
Valley Journal

ASK, AND IT IS GIVEN?

Well. That didn't get me very far. Additionally, the response is very poorly written, especially having come from the editorial department of the paper.

I morosely deleted the message. I checked to see if I received any responses from family or friends. I had not.

"James Edward! I need to speak to you this instant!" Diane sounded rather perturbed.

* * *

So much for family and friends.

Diane had received phone calls all day complaining of my email.

"Do you know how embarrassing this is?" She stood in front of me with her hands planted firmly upon her hips.

I didn't respond. I pushed my spectacles up my nose. I blinked back my tears.

This isn't working out so well.

"Everyone thinks we're rolling in money because your father is a lawyer. Do you know what they think now?"

"No, Ma'am." And, I didn't.

"They have the impression you're a gold-digger without manners. I'm wondering if they're right." Diane's face was scarlet.

Her eyes blazed, then she lowered her head.

"Wait, I didn't mean that." She let out an audible sigh.

"I know your heart was in the right place. But, darn it, James! You just can't go around asking people for money. Please understand. People will give you their time, or their belongings... but money is a totally different thing. When you ask for their money, they... well, they don't like it and they don't trust it. And, they don't trust anyone who asks for a hand-out."

"That doesn't make very much sense. It's just money." I sniffled.

I pushed my spectacles harder into my face to hide my tears. I kept my hair covering my eyes for the same reason. I had to fight the urge to brush it away, though.

"No, it doesn't, but that's the way people are. They think... They think they work hard for their money. They don't part with money easily, or without a fight. Unless they get something in return. Some kind of reward; a tangible object... like a TV or car... or at least accolades and some sort of acknowledgement for their unselfish act or monetary gift.

"But to give anonymously? No way. Not very often, anyway." The anger seemed to wash away from Diane's face, and sadness replaced it.

"But, what about Jones? Wouldn't it make them feel virtuous assisting her, even anonymously?"

"No... Quite frankly, no. Oh, James, it's a strange world we live in." Diane knelt down beside me and brushed my bangs to the side. She kissed my forehead and smiled at me.

"I don't understand it myself sometimes," she said. "Please promise me you won't ask for anymore hand-outs. Please?"

"Yes, Diane. I promise. No more asking."

ASK, AND IT IS GIVEN.

Not so much.

✎ Chapter Five ✐

ALL THAT GLITTERS

"Okay. It's all set. Grandfather is, like, coming over today and tomorrow to help me mum bake all of the food. He's going to stop by your place to pick up the groceries first. Gonza, I just hope they get me kitchen all cleaned up before school lets out."

We stood outside the school. We waited for the morning bell to chime. Jones had excused herself to go to the restroom. It gave us ample opportunity to discuss our plans.

"I put the ingredients on the rear porch. It's chilly enough the perishable items will survive. Did you inform Grandfather where to locate them?"

"Sure did. Crikey, I have to say all this sneaking around is kinda fun. Are you guys having as much fun?"

"I had some serious set-backs yesterday with my other idea. I think we're back on track now." I kicked the snow from my boot.

"What kind of set-backs?" Buck inquired.

"Nothing of importance. Shhh. Here she comes." I hoped they wouldn't bring it up again. I felt my cheeks grow hot thinking about the conversation I had with Diane the previous night.

Jones entered our group. She tried to smile.

"Hey."

"Hey, Jones. Did everything come out okay?" Buck inquired.

"That's just grosser than a pug-dog with a head cold." Jones smiled then, though. The bell chimed.

* * *

Something Diane had declared the night before woke me from a sound sleep early Thursday night.

Gold digger.

She said our family and friends think I'm a gold digger. So, if the shoe fits...

I couldn't wait to get to school on Friday. As I headed out the door, Don halted me.

"Hey, Little Man, I think you should rethink your shoe choice."

I glanced down. My gym shoe clothed my right foot. My dress shoe enveloped my left.

"Is it 'mismatch day' at school?" Ron inquired. "I remember when we had those. That was kinda fun. Maybe we should ask Principle Barkley if..."

"No, fellas. It's not." I ran upstairs. I replaced the dress shoe with my other gym shoe. I detested wearing boots to school unless it had recently snowed.

I ran downstairs. I bolted out the door. I caught up with Ron and Don. They were just gaining access to their vehicle.

"Hey, fellas. Can I request a favor?"

"Sure, Little Man, you can ask. But, I can't promise anything." Don replied.

Ron tussled my hair. He pushed me away.

"Can one of you fellas give Buck and me a ride out to Sinks Canyon tomorrow morning?"

"You want to go look for that mine, don't cha?" Ron laughed. "It's just a silly tale, you know? It doesn't exist, 'cept in Uncle Ivan's head. He was just entertaining us. Jax said so."

"Just the same, will you fellas?"

"Sure. I've been wanting to check it out, too. Even though Ron's pestering you, he hasn't shut-up about it since." Don sat in the driver's seat. He left his door open to talk with me.

"Hey!" Ron climbed into the front passenger's seat. He slammed his door.

"Hey, yourself, Ron. James, tell Buck to meet us at the end of his drive at 7:00 am sharp. Pack a lunch and a drink. We'll make a day of it." Don shut his car door. He waved as they pulled out of the drive.

I waved back.

I headed off to school with notions of finding tons of gold. Hopefully, ample gold to get Jones to her parents.

* * *

"How'd the baking go?" Buck whispered to Blue over the lunch table. Jones was up getting a juice. The lunch lady was taking much time in retrieving it from the back cooler.

"'Tastic. Me mum said the cookies and the brownies are done. They have the pies ready to bake today. Right before they go out this afternoon, they're going to fry the scone-thingies.

"They're best hot, Grandfather says. I guess they made some cinnamon honey-butter to put on them, too," Buck interjected.

Blue licked her lips and rubbed her belly.

"It's no less than brilliant! Me mum is going to, like, go door-to-door this weekend, too. She'll sell what she can. Then on Monday, she'll hit the businesses in town."

"Crikey, Blue, she'll not spill what the sale is for, will she?"

"Give us a break, Buck. No! She's thinking if it works out, though, she might make it a home business."

"Cool. Grandfather won't say anything, either. He's jazzed about it, too. He enjoys baking. It's his favorite hobby. Teaching your mom *Inuna-Ina* ways pleases him."

Jones walked up to the table. She set the juice down. "Well, that took longer than a Catholic wedding."

"Glad to have you back, Jones. However, we're finished here, so..." I started to get up.

"Don't y'all even think of leavin' here 'til I'm done with my food. Hear me?"

"Sir, yes, Sir!" Blue sat up straight in her seat. She saluted Jones. Buck and I followed suit. Then, we all cracked up laughing, including Jones.

* * *

Buck stood at the end of his drive. He sprinted to our vehicle as we arrived. His knapsack appeared to be chock-full of food and drinks. Probably some of Grandfather's buffalo jerky was in there.

"Hey, Buck," Don stated. Buck got into the back seat with me.

"Hey, guys. Hey, JEEP. I brought you guys dried dog meat." Buck smiled. He tossed his knapsack on the floor.

"That's just not amusing," I replied.

"Travis didn't think so, either." Ron burst into laughter. Don chuckled.

"How do you guys know about that?" Buck inquired.

"Who doesn't know about that? It was all over the school the next day." Don replied. "Good job, fellas."

"Jones and Blue told Travis it was dog meat. I thought it was pretty funny, though, too." Buck snickered. "Served him right."

I spotted Billy Bump Hill from my window.

We were nearly there.

I sensed excitement rise inside me.

"Can we investigate the cabin first?" I inquired.

"Absolutely!" Don replied.

* * *

It stood before us, broken down and uninhabitable. I wasn't sure if we could gain entrance. Don handed us each a flashlight.

"We might need these," he stated.

Ron found a passage under the crushed and tumbled tin roof. I carefully followed him in. The displeasing stench of stale beer and wood-rot greeted my nose.

After making my way through the wrecked entrance, I was able to stand upright. The hardwood floor crumbled in areas underfoot. However, the old cabin walls were stable enough. I held onto them as I ambled through the one-roomed shack.

I flipped my flashlight to the on position. Buck flicked on his. Then, my brothers followed suit. The room lit up with four moving beams. My light illuminated an old, rusted box spring, visible through a large window to our west. It leaned up against the outside of the cabin.

"That's to keep the bears out," Don stated. "I haven't seen a bear this far down the mountain, ever. But I guess it must have been a problem when the old man lived here. All the windows are like that. See?"

The roof and floor showed signs of a now-gone wood-burning stove and stovepipe. Empty, uncovered cupboards lined the east wall. There were two stained and torn mattresses in the far corner. Numerous empty beer and wine bottles littered the place. There wasn't really anything spectacular at which to gaze.

Years before someone must have liberated anything worth attention. It just looked like an old, worn-down cabin, now used irresponsibly by delinquent high school kids.

Don picked up an old, rusted tin can. He read the top and laughed.

"HA! I guess it *is* all relative!" He tossed the can to me.

What it had once contained was impossible for me to discern. The top had two, triangular piercings from an old-time bottle opener. Barely legible writing on the top stated: 'HAMMS. New Aluminum Top. Easy To Open.'

I chuckled, and handed it to Ron.

I turned to leave through the rubble tunnel. The floorboards gave way a bit. I grabbed the top of the broken door frame to steady myself. I felt indentations in the wood.

I shone my flashlight on it.

"Hey, fellas, look at this."

Carved into the log was:

TOM BLANKENSHIP + BILL SHANAHAN

OCT 25, 19...

The year was indecipherable.

"What do you make of that?" Ron asked.

—"I'm not sure. It rings a bell, though. Bill Shanahan. I've heard that name somewhere before." Don scratched his head in thought.

"Well, it'll eventually come to me. Let's get to that mine so we have enough time to explore. The Weather Channel said snow today. I hope it was wrong."

We hiked up to the top of the hill. We spotted what looked like used to be a mine shaft.

Railroad tracks penetrated the floor of the ruptured mine. Oily railroad ties held up its right half. I shined my flashlight into the small opening.

I couldn't see much.

"Hey! Here's that drain pipe Uncle Ivan told us about," Ron stated. He indicated the long pipe running down the side of the mountain. Water poured from its rusted mouth in a steady stream. A strong smell like rotten eggs emitted from the pipe.

I peered back into the shaft. My heart sunk to my knees. All hope of finding gold vanished with the appearance of the dilapidated mine.

I shone my light on the floor of the mine. I swept it across the rubble. Something dull and square caught my eye.

"Hey, fellas. What do you suppose that is?"

"What is it, James? What do you see?" Don inquired.

"That." I gestured with my flashlight.

"I don't see anything." Ron scrunched down to my eye level. "What are you talking about?"

"That. Right there. Don't you fellas see it? That little square. It looks like it might be... a wallet?"

Just then, the Weather Channel was proven correct.

It began to snow.

Hard.

๏ Chapter Six ๏

WORTH DYING FOR

"Do you think you can reach it?" Don sounded concerned.

"Yeah, just." I was on my hands and knees, crawling through the mine's opening. My coat caught.

I lowered myself onto my belly. I snake-crawled a little further. Some gravel and dust sifted down on top of me.

"Careful, little bro. I don't want to explain to Mom how you died today," Don stated.

"Don't worry, you won't have to. Besides, if it caves in, just leave me. Eugene and Diane have too many kids anyway. They won't miss me. They can just adopt another son." I talked as I crawled.

I stopped every inch to make sure the walls didn't collapse on my back.

"Is JEEP adopted?" I heard Buck ask my brothers.

"Yep. We all are," Ron stated. "Why do you think there are so many of us?"

"Never really thought about it. JEEP just never mentioned it before..."

"Hey, I think I can reach it. Hold on. Yep, I think it's a..."

Just then, the left wall of the mine gave way. Something hard and big landed on my back.

It knocked the wind out of me. My eyes smoked over in pain. I couldn't breathe.

I couldn't breathe!

Help me, I can't breathe. Darkness surrounded me. My world spun.

"Hey move this! We gotta get him outta there!" Voices drifted into my ears through what seemed to be a back door.

"Hold his leg! On the count of three!"

"Forget that! PULL!"

I felt my body float over the gravel earth. I could see a tunnel of light.

Go toward the light. Aren't you always supposed to go toward the light? I don't wanna die yet. Please, God, not yet.

My lungs filled with air. The light grew brighter. My body rolled over. I felt little cold kisses on my face.

"Tell Momma I love her."

"Tell her yourself, you little freak." Ron's voice was shaky.

I opened my eyes. I tried to sit up. However, my chest hurt immensely.

"I'm not dead? I'm not dead! OUCH!" It hurt to talk.

"That was a stupid thing for us to do." Don paced back in forth in the falling snow.

He ran his hand through his hair. I could practically hear his heart beating from where I lay.

"What an idiot! Mom would have killed me. Ron, I don't know why I let you talk me into having James crawl through that hole. He coulda been..."

"He's the only one small enough to fit. Well, would you look at that! The little freak got it." Ron pointed at my hand.

Clutched in my battered hand, was an old, brown leather wallet. I couldn't move. I just lay there. I looked at it, then at Don.

He hunkered down.

"You okay, Little Man?" Don pulled my spectacles from my face.

"Yeah."

"You sure? Can you sit up?" He wiped my spectacles on his shirt. He put them back on my face. They were a little crooked.

Luckily, they didn't appear to be broken, or scratched.

"No."

Don reached over and pulled the wallet from my hand. He put it in his coat pocket. He slipped his hand under my back. He gently raised me into a sitting position. My bottom started to feel the cold. I assumed that was a good sign. I felt extreme pain in my ribcage. I tried to take in a deep breath. A sharp twinge stabbed my chest.

"Ow, it hurts," I whispered. I felt the tears forming. I tried to blink them away. Crying would only make the pain worse.

"We need to get him to the doctor's." Don picked me up.

Each step he took toward the vehicle felt like a dagger in my side. I tried holding my breath. It seemed like a much longer trip back, than up.

"Ron! Take the keys from my right coat pocket. You're driving."

Buck ran over to the car. He opened the car door for Don.

"Hey, JEEP, how ya doing?" Buck asked.

I tried to smile. However, I don't know how it came across. Buck's face looked peculiar. He stepped back to let Don pass.

Ron sat behind the steering wheel. He turned the key in the ignition.

Whrrr... Whrr... Whrrr...

"What's going on? Stupid thing, start!" Ron struck the wheel with his fist. He turned the key again.

"The engine's not gonna turn over, bro." Ron sighed heavily. "What now?"

"Let's carry him to the nearest house. Maybe they can call an ambulance. Dang! I wish we had a cell phone." Don climbed out of the car with me in his arms.

Every step he took made my side feel like it was going to crack open and spill my guts everywhere.

"Hey, there's a house." Buck pointed across the street. I saw smoke rising from the chimney. Snow fell hard. The fresh, white crystals covered the ground. The world looked like a painting. I felt faint.

"No way, man. That's Old Lady Shanahan's. She gives me the creeps with all her cats. I don't care if she is Dad and Mom's friend. She's just plain weird." Ron shook his head emphatically. "My vote is we're not going there!"

Shanahan. The name sounds familiar. I closed my eyes.

"We have to, Ron. James is small, but he's not that small. I don't know how much longer I can carry him. The next nearest house is over a mile down the road."

"Help you boys?" Old Lady Shanahan stood at her door. She peered through a crack just wide enough for us to see a sliver of her face. She had answered the door after the second knock.

"Mrs. Shanahan, my brother's been hurt. Our car won't start. Can we use your phone to call our dad?"

Mrs. Shanahan stared at Don for a bit, and then looked at me. Her one visible eye rotated in its socket. It went from Don to me, then back to Don. After what seemed to be eternity, she finally recognized Don. She opened the door a bit wider.

"Heavens to Betsy, Donald. What happened to him?" Her hair sat on top of her head, tucked tightly in a bun. Pieces of hair had escaped, though. It left her looking a tad wild. Her face was as wrinkled as Grandfather's. She had a look of sadness to her.

A cat escaped through the opened door. It skittered down the snowy path. Mrs. Shanahan ran out after it.

"Now look what you've gone and done. Tabitha! Come back here! Gonna catch your death." Mrs. Shanahan turned back to us. "She'll be back. Might as well let you in, afore the rest get out. Take a look at your boy. What'say happened?"

"We were up at the old mine..."

"Heavens child! Your father know you take your kid brother near that old death trap?" Her eyes blazed with crazy.

She reached out and snatched me from Don's arms. She laid me on her couch. It was covered with... cat hair? Ew. However, it felt better to lay still on a hard surface. She prodded and poked at me.

"Know what I'm doing. Used to be a nurse." Mrs. Shanahan talked in incomplete

386 ~ The Elementary Adventures of Jones, JEEP, Buck & Blue

sentences. None-the-less, I had no trouble understanding her.

"Boy's got cracked ribs," she said, matter-of-factly, like it happened every day. "Lucky not fractured completely. Can't call, though. Phone isn't working. Went down. Don't know how long. No signal." She gestured to me. "Which one is he?"

"James," Don responded.

The power in the old house flickered and went out, then came back on. Then it went out and didn't come back on.

"No power 'til morn, no doubt. Might as well settle in."

Mrs. Shanahan's home was an old, well-built cabin. It was one large room with three doors in the back, near the kitchen area. It had a fireplace in the corner of the front. A large witch's cauldron-type pot hung over the flames. I heard something bubble inside it.

Mrs. Shanahan walked over to the fire-place. She grabbed a long match from the mantel. She caught the match with the fire and lit candles throughout the house. A comfortable glow filled the home.

That's when I noticed the smell. A warm, meaty aroma filled my nostrils. Stew. Yummy stew. And, something else. A sharp, putrid smell. Cats! Stew and cats!

Oh, please God, not stewed cats!

I felt a soft thud on my legs. I looked down to see a small kitten licking its paw. Then, I saw another cat looking down on me from the back of the couch.

Just how many felines does this old woman have?

"Knew the power was going. Been flickerin' all day. Started the stew a bit ago. Enough to last all week." Mrs. Shanahan went back to the pot and stirred it.

"No worries. I'll share," she said.

She walked back to me. She placed a warm, soft hand on my head. I felt immediately comforted. "You doin' okay, James?"

I nodded.

"Sit." She gestured to the fellas. "Anywhere there's no cat."

Don and Ron sat on the couch's armrests, on either side of me. Buck sat on the edge of a wooden rocker's seat. Nobody had dared to say anything. They all looked very frightened to me.

"Hungry?"

"No Ma'am." Don cleared his throat. "Thank you."

"You will be. So, tell me. Why up at the mine?"

She sat in the rocker opposite Buck. She looked from me, to Don, to Ron and then to Buck. She waited for one of us to speak up.

Buck did.

"We heard about it from their uncle. We wanted to see if it really existed."

"It does. Curiosity dealt with? Had enough? Won't be going back now, will ya?"

"No Ma'am, I mean, yes, Ma'am. I mean, we won't be going back," Don stammered.

"Except to get our car," Ron added.

"Well, get that shirt off your boy. Gotta wrap the ribs. Go now." Mrs. Shanahan arose from her seat.

She walked briskly to one of the doors in the back. When she opened it, I could see an old, claw-foot tub. The bathroom. She came back out with an ace-bandage and a wet washcloth. Don jumped up. He carefully removed my coat, then my shirt. I tried not to wince, however I did anyway.

"Sorry, Little Man. I'm trying to be gentle."

"'S okay," I said, blinking back tears. The

pain was immense. When I stayed static, the ache lessened.

Mrs. Shanahan walked into the kitchen. She grabbed a bottle of something and a glass of water. Then, she came back to me.

"Allergic?"

"No, not that I know," Don stated. He stepped back out of her way.

Mrs. Shanahan put the bottle and glass on the end-table. She laid the washcloth across my forehead. The coolness felt delicious. She effortlessly wrapped my chest with the gauze. When she finished, I felt better.

"You sit?"

"I can try," I whispered. I found it easier now that she'd wrapped me like a cocoon. I still had to move slowly, though. She handed me a pill and the glass of water.

"Take this. Ibuprofen. Helps with the pain. Then, lay back."

I did as she said.

I closed my eyes and started to drift. I heard voices through the back door of my head again. I couldn't make out what was being said.

"Where did you say you found this?!"

The shrillness of Mrs. Shanahan's voice woke me. I looked to see her holding the wallet I had pulled from the mine. Her hands were shaking fiercely.

"The mine. James grabbed it just as the walls caved in on him." Ron stated.

"Stupid thing to do," Mrs. Shanahan whispered. She turned the wallet over in her hands. She seemed unable to open it.

"Have you opened it?" She inquired of Don. "Do you know to whom it belongs?"

"No. I just shoved it into my pocket. Then, came here to get help for James," Don stated.

Mrs. Shanahan handed the wallet back to Don. "I think you'll find it belonged to my son, Bill."

Bill Shanahan! On the wall of the cabin!

Don opened the wallet. Fine dust spilt out over the rug and couch. He looked up apologetically.

"Go on," Mrs. Shanahan said, her face pale. Her hands gripped the rocker's armrests.

Don pulled out an old, brittle library card. "William Shanahan." He looked up, a bit startled. "Mrs. Shanahan! Are you alright?"

Ron jumped up and ran to the old woman's side. She had collapsed in her chair.

"Buck, hand me that glass of water! Don, grab the washcloth from James' head!" Ron felt for Mrs. Shanahan's pulse. He blotted her face with the cloth.

"Mrs. Shanahan, can you hear me? Are you okay?"

ço $ ૭ઌ

๑ Chapter Seven ๑

IT'S ALL RELATIVE

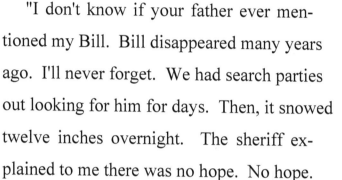

"I don't know if your father ever mentioned my Bill. Bill disappeared many years ago. I'll never forget. We had search parties out looking for him for days. Then, it snowed twelve inches overnight. The sheriff explained to me there was no hope. No hope. But, I never really gave up. I prayed he had run away and that someday he'd come back to my door. He never did." Mrs. Shanahan sniffled loudly. She blew her nose into a tissue.

"I told him over and over again to stay away from that silly mine." Mrs. Shanahan turned the wallet over in her hand. She smoothed its surface. She stroked it as if it was her son's cheek. She lifted it up to her nose and smelled deeply the aroma of the old leather.

"Still smells a little like him," she stated. She kissed the wallet gently.

"When did Bill disappear?" Don inquired. His face looked a tad weird.

"In October. I'll never forget. It was a Saturday... or maybe Sunday... could have been Friday, but I'll never forget the date. October 25th."

All of us sucked in air at the same time. I looked at Don, then to Ron, then to Buck. They all had the same look on their faces.

Don finally gathered up enough courage to ask the question we all wanted to know. "Uh, Mrs. Shanahan, was, uh, Bill friends with Tom Blankenship?"

"Never liked that boy. A bully if you ask me. Grew up to be a sheriff's deputy, I hear.

What a moron, but yes, I caught him hanging around every now and again. Told Bill I didn't much care for him. Told Bill I saw nothing but badness in that boy. Told him he'd end up dead, or worse. But what's a mother to do? Kid's gonna run with whomever runs with him. Why do you ask?"

"No reason, really." Don looked at us with a look that read to me 'don't say anything until we know more.' "I just remember hearing through the years that they were friends."

"At the time, Sheriff Richie, now, he was a fine man. Anyhow, Sheriff Richie thought Tom had something to do with Bill's disappearance. But, Tom denied it. Said he hadn't seen Bill in weeks. I don't know, though. I always thought something was hanky-panky there. Are any of you boys hungry yet?"

The smell of stew hit my nose again. My stomach growled loudly.

"I can tell this youngster is," Mrs. Shanahan pointed at me. "I'll fix you each a bowl.
Then, we'll discuss how reckless it was of you
to visit that mine. And, then you can enligh-
ten me as to what's so all-fire important
enough you can risk your lives over. Apparently, my boy shared your curiosity."

The stew meat melted in my mouth. The
gravy coated my tongue with flavor. I didn't
even mind the carrots. It was the best beef
stew I had ever tasted.

I soaked up the remaining gravy with a
dinner roll. I licked my fingers.

"Dang, James. You never eat like that at
home," Ron stated. I just smiled.

Mrs. Shanahan brought out some chocolate
cake. She cut us each a large piece.

A faint memory of a witch fattening up
some small children to eat came to mind. I
pushed it away.

The cake was delicious, so I told her so.

"The cake is delicious."

"Thank you, James. Now explain to me what you were doing up there."

I repeated Uncle Ivan's tale of the gold. I explained why Buck and I were looking for it. Buck started to object as I began, but he relaxed a bit when I didn't give any particulars.

Ron and Don listened intently. They hadn't heard that part of the story. When I finished, Mrs. Shanahan had a very sad look on her face.

"I recently lost a nephew in that war. My heart goes out to your friend. I hope you find a way to get her to her dad."

"Well, without the gold, I don't know how we're going to do that," Buck stated.

"Mrs. Shanahan, can I try your phone? It's getting really late. I'm afraid Mom will be worried about us," Don stated.

Mrs. Shanahan walked to the wall phone and picked up it up. She listened into it. Her face brightened.

"Young man, it seems to be working." She held the phone out to Don. "The power will soon follow."

Don took the receiver and dialed.

I felt relieved. Mrs. Shanahan had been a proper host. She was not at all as scary as I'd feared. However, I really wanted to see Diane. My ribs began to throb again.

I need Diane's comforting arms. I would never say that aloud, however.

"Mom said Dad is on his way. She said she'd call Grandfather and let him know you're okay, Buck." Don turned to Mrs. Shanahan. "She said she's very grateful to you as always. If there's anything she can do..."

"Pish-posh. You tell her never mind. It's

my pleasure. And, now maybe I can get some answers about Bill's disappearance. Thanks to that wallet you found. You didn't find anything else, did you?"

"No, Ma'am," Ron replied.

Just then, Mrs. Shanahan's lights flickered on. The room brightened with candles and electric lights.

"Help me blow out these candles, will you, boys?"

* * *

"Dad, can I see you outside?" Don stood at the door. Eugene had conferred my injuries with Mrs. Shanahan. The pleasantries were coming to an end.

"Sure thing, Son." Eugene turned to me. "James, I'll be right back to carry you to the car. The rest of you wait here. Don and I are going to try to get that car started."

The door shut behind them.

I started walking around the room. The second Tylenol was taking effect. The pain in my chest was easing.

Mrs. Shanahan had family photos on all the walls of her cabin. Some were very old. Others were more recent. I started at the old ones. They were sepia-toned and ancient-looking. I walked gingerly around the room. I happened upon a photo of a young boy in his teens, with an older man.

"That's Bill with his father, my Walter." Mrs. Shanahan's voice made me jump a tad. She stood behind me.

"Walter left us the summer before Bill disappeared. I took this right before Walter died. From the cancer. Bill was just 15 there. He missed his father greatly. For awhile, I thought I had done something to make him leave." Mrs. Shanahan sighed heavily. I saw tears welling in her old, watery eyes.

She put her arm around me and said, "I don't think you know what a comfort you boys are to me, finding Bill's wallet and all. No such thing as coincidence, you know. I've been asking for some sort of sign for awhile now. I don't think I'll be here much longer. It'll be nice to put Bill to rest before I go."

ASK, AND IT IS GIVEN

"This one here. You should recognize that boy." Mrs. Shanahan pointed to a framed snapshot of two boys in their teens. The boy on the left was Bill, looking not much older than in the previous picture. A boy stood on the right, with his arm across Bill's shoulders. It was a younger version of Eugene.

"Is that Eugene... uh, my father?"

"He has always been such a blessing to my family." Mrs. Shanahan walked away from me. She wiped her eyes.

I continued looking at pictures down the

wall. I was almost to the end when one more photo caught my eye.

"Hey, Buck. Take a gander at this."

Buck walked up to me.

He examined at the photo I indicated. It was a picture of a woman holding an infant boy. A young red-haired girl sat beside them. A man, with hair as red as hers, stood over them. The family was complete. They looked pleasant and happy.

"Wow. Is that who I think it is?" Buck inquired.

"I think so."

"That's my nephew with his family. They just moved here. Well, his family did. I told you my nephew recently died in the war."

Mrs. Shanahan walked over to us. She lovingly touched the man's face. "He was such a nice man; my Walter's sister's boy. His name was David Blumenthal."

It was the first time either Buck or I had seen a picture of Blue's father.

"So, you, uh, you're Aunt Nan?" I asked.

"Why, yes, young man, I am." She had a strange look on her face.

"You're Blue's, uh, Jessica's Aunt?" Buck inquired.

"Do you two know my little Jessie?"

"Yes, very well. She's our friend," I stated. "Jones, I mean, Suzanna and Jessica are our very good friends. In fact, Suzanna is the one who needs to get to Washington, DC to see her father."

"Why, Jessie never told me Suzanna's father was in a bad way." Mrs. Shanahan's face contorted.

"Please, Mrs. Shanahan, please don't tell anyone we told you. Jessica made us promise not to tell. Please." Buck pleaded with Mrs. Shanahan.

"Yes, please." I added.

"Your secret is safe with me, young men. It's nice to know Jessie has good friends like you." Mrs. Shanahan smiled warmly. She squeezed my hand. "My Bill had one good friend in Gene, too."

The front door opened. We turned to see Eugene enter. Don followed. Eugene had a peculiar look on his face. I knew Don had shown him the names carved in the cabin wall.

"Car's running fine. Ron, you and Buck go with Don. Don will drop Buck off on the way home. I'm taking James to the clinic to be checked out." Eugene turned to Mrs. Shanahan. "Nan, thanks for all your help. Again, I owe you. I hope I'll be able to return a favor to you someday." Eugene held out his arms in an embrace. "I have some things to check out, but you can be assured I will call you shortly."

Mrs. Shanahan walked into the hug. She returned the embrace.

"Thanks, Gene. You were always a great friend to Bill. To me." She stepped away. She wiped her eyes. "Give Diane my love."

Driving to the clinic, I found the words to ask Eugene something on my mind.

"Eugene, were you really Bill Shanahan's friend?"

"He was my best friend, James. We were barely 16 when he disappeared. It felt like my whole world disappeared along with him. Mrs. Shanahan helped me through some very dark times."

"I think you helped her, too."

"More than that, James. Mrs. Shanahan took me in when my parents died in a car crash, just a few months after Bill vanished."

Eugene cleared his throat, and then continued. "She helped me with college tuition and through graduate school. I didn't even have to ask. If it weren't for her love and kindness back then, I wouldn't be a lawyer today. We owe so much to her."

"So, how come I've never met her?"

At first, I didn't think he heard me because he didn't answer. Just when I was about to repeat my question, he once again cleared his throat and spoke. His voice sounded peculiar.

"You have met her. You were just too young to remember. She held you the first day we brought you home. She hasn't been over much in the past five or six years.

"We should have her over more often. When your mother and I first got married, she came to dinner nightly. Then, Harrison came into our lives, and she was always there. She loved that boy. He's named after Bill, you know? Harrison William.

"We got busy. Life got in the way. I call

her once a month, but..."

A long silence followed his words.

Finally, I spoke what was secondary on my mind.

"Eugene, you know how I feel about God and such?"

"Yeah?"

"Well, when I was in that mine and the walls caved in on me, I found myself praying for God to let me live. I can't explain it. Why did I do that? I don't believe in God."

"Some people believe in something greater than themselves - some unknown force. Some outer knowledge that leads and protects them. Others put a face and form to that something. They go to church to worship. And, still others know that force is within each of them. And, whether we pray to a being on a throne, or to a cloud of oneness, or within, our prayers are heard and answered." Eugene looked at me through the rearview mirror. "It's human nature to ask for assistance, especially in dire times."

"Does that mean deep down I do believe in God?"

"Maybe... on some level. You know, James, you can believe in God without being religious. Or, labeled as a Christian, or Mormon, or Catholic, or Jewish, whatever the label. You can be spiritual. Even if our depiction of GOD is just a way to keep us culturally, ethically bound, is that such a bad thing? I can think of worse."

A vision of Tom Blankenship blazed through my mind.

Travis stood behind him.

They each had the same, crazy look in their eyes.

An icy shiver ran down my spine.

∽ $ ∾

❧ Chapter Eight ❧
ONLY WHEN I LAUGH

"Gonza! Me Aunt Nan didn't say you got hurt this bad." Blue walked into my bedroom. Jones followed closely behind her.

Jones clutched a wilted carnation. She held it out to me. "Here. I was fixin' to get to the flower shop, but Mrs. B is as busy as a... Wow! You looked bunged up!"

"Thanks, Jones." I took the purple blossom she offered.

"I didn't know you knew me Aunt Nan."

"I wasn't aware I knew your aunt, either. I discovered just yesterday she's Eugene's God-mother."

"Small world." Blue said, as she sat at the end of my bed.

"Why aren't you attending church today, Jones?" I inquired.

Jones shrugged. "Don't know. Prayin' seems to be as useless as a bucket in a flood." Her bottom lip started to tremble.

Words eluded me. I kept quiet.

Blue fidgeted on the bed. She examined her hands as if she'd never noticed them before.

An uncomfortable silence filled my room.

"Ron told me you guys were up here." Buck's voice entered the room a step before he did. "What's up?"

Buck stopped when he saw me; bandaged and wrapped from hip to wrist.

"Crikey, JEEP! You didn't look this bad yesterday. What'd the doctors do to you?"

"Four cracked ribs, bruised right scapula and sprained right carpal. Plus, they think I may have suffered a mild concussion."

"Could be worse." Buck sat at my computer chair and smiled.

"Gonza, Buck. What could be worse than a brain injury?"

"You could be one of the Blankenship boys." Buck grinned so wide it looked as if his face would split open.

"Spill!" Blue grabbed Buck's arm.

"Grandfather said last night your dad reported the writing we found in the cabin, and the wallet from the mine to the police."

"Go on," Blue urged.

"The old goldmine that collapsed on you... Hey, how come you never said anything about you and your siblings being adopted?"

"Never gave it much thought. Why? Does it make a difference?" I waited for the answer.

More so, I waited for more queries.

"I don't know. Just nice to know. Anyway, the police excavated that old mine this very morning. They found the skeletal remains of one William Shanahan."

Blue and Jones sucked in all the air from the room, which was quite okay. A sharp intake of breath was not an option for me.

"Cousin Bill?" Blue's jaw dropped. "Wait, JEEP's adopted?"

"Dang!" I realized my jaw hung open as well. I closed my mouth.

"There's more," Buck continued. "After seeing that carving on the cabin wall, the police questioned Deputy Blankenship. He started blubbering and spilled the whole story.

"It seems that back when they were teenagers, Deputy Tom Blankenship goaded Bill Shanahan into going up to the mine to look for gold. Tom said he really just wanted to talk to Bill.

"They got into a scuffle inside the mine - fought over some girl named Lenore, the now

Mrs. Blankenship. That's when they think Bill's wallet fell out of his pocket. While they fought.

"I don't know why anyone would fight over a girl, especially any girl who would marry a Blankenship. But, anyway, Tom pushed Bill. Bill fell down a vertical shaft."

"Wow. That's what killed Bill?" I asked.

"No. Tom said he tried to reach Bill. But, Bill was too far down, and treading water. So, Tom told Bill he was going to get some rope or something. As Tom left the mine, he supposedly tripped on a rock, or ledge, or something.

"He hit the support on the left side of the opening. He knocked the railroad tie out of place. The mine collapsed. Tom ran home and never went back."

"Gonza. He left Cousin Bill in there, like, to die?"

"Looks like it. Police could somehow tell by Bill's remains that he starved to death – plenty of water, but no food. They're holding Tom Blankenship on suspicion of murder. But, that's not all."

"There's even more?" Jones inquired.

"We were all wrong, JEEP. We said it wouldn't be the last time we saw Travis," Buck stated.

"So?" I responded.

"Travis punched out a police officer when they were putting cuffs on his dad. Got himself taken away as well. He's going away for a very long time."

Buck's smile grew bigger, if that was possible. "He won't be messing with me... us anymore. See, there is a God, after all."

"Don't count on it." Jones' bottom lip trembled again. Buck's last words had turned Jones' face back into a frown.

Blue got up and put her arm around Jones.

"You know, Jones, when me dad died, you said God answers all of our prayers. I know you and I have a different idea of whom or what God is. But, if you want me to pray with you for your father, I will. We all will."

I felt uncomfortable. I hadn't ever prayed before. Unless you count what I did after the mine collapsed on top of me.

"Do y'all know all about Dad?" Jones looked at me. She looked at Buck. Then, she fixed her glare on Blue.

"You wasn't supposed to snitch. You promised."

"Gonza, Jones, I didn't want to promise. They have a bloody right to know anyway. They're your friends, too. And, we were really trying to find a way to help you." Blue replied. "If you want to pray, we can. Just tell us what you want us to do."

"We could do the sacred Sun Dance ceremony. *Inuna-Ina* believe if we fast for four days and four nights, and pray to the Creator, our prayers will be heard and answered." Buck interjected.

Ask, and it is given...

I knew I didn't have any answers. I wanted to find a way to get Jones back with her parents. I had asked my friends and family and community for help, for all the good it did.

"So much for 'ask, and it is given'," I stated.

"Oh, that reminds me." Blue talked fast with excitement. "I asked me mum what that book was about. She said it's about making your wishes come true by trusting they will. She said it's a four step process." Blue counted off the steps with her fingers.

"'Decide what you want. Believe you can have it. Believe you deserve it. Believe it's possible for you.'" Blue paused only long enough to take a breath.

"Then, me mum said to close your eyes for a few minutes every day. Then, pretend you already have it. Then, think about what you have that you're already thankful for."

"Bonus. Thanksgiving's the time for that." Jones interjected. Her voice was peculiarly flat. "What're y'all thankful for?"

"I'm thankful our Creator took care of Travis and his dad," Buck stated. "Things are going to be a lot better without him in my life." He did the birthday dance again.

"I'm thankful I didn't die in that mine like William Shanahan." I shuddered, causing my sides to hurt. "I'm thankful my friend and brothers didn't run out on me."

"I'm thankful me Aunt Nan found her son after all these years. She's a much more peaceful soul knowing what happened to Bill."

"I know I oughtta be thankful, but right now I'm catchin' myself feelin' sadder than... well, nothin's sadder." Jones sniffed loudly. "Blue, can we get on home? Momma's fixin' to call in a bit."

"Sure, Jones. Let's go." Blue took Jones' hand. "Hey, JEEP, I hope you feel better. Bye, Buck."

"See you guys," Buck stated. We watched the two girls leave my room, as tears trickled down Jones' cheeks.

"I wish we could do something for her. I wasn't kidding about the Sun Dance." Buck looked down at the floor. "Have any ideas?"

"No. Not really. I suppose we could try the steps Blue recited. You know, visualize and believe and all."

"You wanna?"

"I don't know how it'll help. I don't think it can hurt, though."

"Okay, then. Close your eyes. This is kinda like the *Inuna-Ina* Vision Quest, but different."

"What are we envisioning?"

"I see Jones running up to a woman in an airport, arms opened wide."

"Yes, I see it, too." I stated.

Wait. How peculiar. I see Blue with her.

* * *

Aunt Nan placed the cooked goose on Grandfather's table and took her seat.

Buck leaned toward me.

"The Blankenships aren't the only ones whose goose is cooked," he whispered in my ear.

I smiled. It still hurt too much to laugh.

"Gene, would you do the honors?" Grandfather asked.

Eugene arose from his seat.

"Wow! What a crowd. And, most of you

came with me!" He smiled and cleared his throat, then continued. "I know we're not an overly-devout family, but due to the circumstances surrounding us being here, I'd like to say a few words.

"William Shanahan's memorial service today reminded me of how precious our connection to friends... good friends and family should be. So, with my wonderful, and large family here around Grandfather's table, sharing this meal with the Blumenthal family and Suzanna, I want to express to all of you how important you are to us, to me. Thank you all for coming and paying your respects to my friend, Bill."

"Gene, may I say something?" Aunt Nan interrupted.

"The floor is yours." Eugene walked over to Aunt Nan. He placed his hand on her shoulder and faced us. Aunt Nan cleared her throat. It looked as though she was having a hard time holding back tears.

"Having Bill back home to rest has been a blessing. One that would've never been, had it not been for these children. I know how important family is this time of year. And, although we heard this morning that Suzanna's father has begun to fight the infection..."

"Crikey, Jones! That's wonderful news," Buck interrupted.

Jones smiled brightly.

Her face flushed scarlet. She looked down at her lap.

Aunt Nan continued.

"And, although he may still lose his leg, he will survive." Aunt Nan stood and walked over to Jones' chair.

"This young woman needs to be with her parents. Therefore, I have arranged for her and Jessie to go to Walter Reed Medical Center to do just that."

A murmur of excitement ran through the group around the table.

"And, because having a husband in the hospital is hard enough, Regina, Charley, and I will travel with the girls to help Susanna's mother. I know a place in Maryland where we can stay."

Jones jumped up and wrapped her arms tightly around the old lady.

Jones' back shook with sobs. Then, she pulled away from Aunt Nan, looked her in the face, and stated, "But... But who all's gonna take care of all them cats?"

The whole group burst into laughter. Everyone, that is, except me. I just smiled.

Blue leaned in toward Buck and me.

"Don't be having any more, like, wild adventures without us."

"We won't," I replied.

"We'll wait until you return," Buck assured her.

Eugene raised his glass.

"To good friends and family. May we all strive to be the best of both."

*Use these questions and activities which follow to get more out of the experience of reading **The Elementary Adventures of Jones, JEEP, Buck & Blue** by Sandra Miller Linhart.*

❧ Literature Circle Questions ❧

1. Why did Blue say she hated her dad if she didn't mean it?

2. Why do you think Jones and her dad joke about his injuries?

3. List three animals Jones and Blue first google on the computer to determine what kind of bones they found in the field? Name two animals they eliminate right away?

4. Why do you think Blue isn't eager to read the letter from her dad?

5. Why do you think the camera failed to take pictures of the meditation stone?

6. If you went on a Vision Quest, what animal totem would you like to have as your guide? How could your choice change your experience? Do you think you'd be afraid of your choice?

7. If you were offered dog meat jerky, would you try it? How do you suppose it would taste? Why?

8. What was in Grandfather's medicine bag? Was it what you thought it would be?

9. Why do you suppose Blue keeps the feather her father gave her with her at all times? Would you keep it with you, or put it in a safe place somewhere? Why?

10. If you saw something strange in the sky, do you think you'd tell anyone? If so, who would you tell? If not, why not?

11. What do believe killed Grandfather's prize bull?

12. Why do you suppose JEEP wasn't afraid of Travis?

13. If you heard about a hidden treasure and went in search of it, would you take anyone with you? Why, or why not?

14. Why did JEEP think Mrs. Shanahan was stewing cats over the fire? Would you eat stewed cats? How do you think it would taste?

15. What would you do if you found a wallet? What if you lost your wallet? Would you want whomever found it to return it to you?

16. JEEP writes "ask, and it is given' on his paper. He asked for money to send Jones to Walter Reed Medical Center, but never received enough money. Do you believe his request granted anyway? Why, or why not?

Activities:

1. When Grandfather is telling the group the *Inuna-Ina* stories of the past, he relates them to present time

situations. Imagine you have traveled forward in time. Write down a story from this time you'd like to pass on to your great-grandchildren. Explain what lessons they might learn from your experiences.

2. Buck calls his grandfather *Nebesiibehe*, which is the *Inuna-Ina* word for grandfather. Using the Internet, find the word "grandfather' in three other languages. Do you believe one language is more important than another? If you could learn only one language other than the one(s) you already know, what would it be? Why?

3. At the end of the series, Jones is to be reunited with her parents in Washington, DC. Do you think her father will lose his leg? Will she stay there while Blue comes back to Wyoming? Write a final chapter describing the outcome.

GLOSSARY OF ACRONYMS & TERMS

ANECDOTE ~ (an-ik-dote) a short account of some interesting or funny event

ARMY BRAT ~ Child of US Army Active Duty Service Member

ASAP ~ As Soon As Possible

BBC ~ British Broadcasting Corporation

BDU ~ Battle Dress Uniform - also Camouflaged Uniform, or Camo

BRAILLE ~ raised dots representing letters and numbers for the blind

CLIPART ~ Brand of computer graphics artwork

IGNEOUS ~ (ig-nē-is) Rocks formed by fire or melted rock

IED ~ Improvised Explosive Device(s). Also known as roadside bombs

GOOGLE ~ a popular Internet search engine; one of many (www.google.com)

LTC ~ Lieutenant Colonel, also called 'Colonel' or Light Colonel

MEDIC ~ Field Military Medical Technician

NATIVE ~ (small n) to be born in

NATIVE AMERICAN ~ American Indian; Original inhabitant of North America

OBSIDIAN ~ (ŏb-sid'ē-in) Black, glass-like volcanic stone

POW-WOWS ~ Social gatherings for celebration, mourning, entertainment and interaction – in full traditional regalia, or garments

TEEPEE ~ (TiPi or Wigwam) Buffalo hides sewn together and wrapped around a circular cone-shaped frame, easily collapsed and transported on a travois. Females of the tribe constructed these homes

TRAVOIS ~ (Tra-Voy) An A-shaped platform. The wider back-end drags on the ground and holds belongings, usually harnessed to dogs and pulled

❧❧NORTHERN ARAPAHO WORDS FOR:

BEETHEI ~ (Băd-hay) Great Grey Owl

BEYOOWU'U ~ (Beh-yaw-wŭ'ŭ) Lodge

CEBETEENOCOO ~ (chep-day-nah-chaw) FryBread

HEBE ~ (heh-beh) greeting among men

HOHÓO ~ (Ha-hoe) Thank you

HONO'IE NEECEEEBI ~ (Haw-nawh'-ī Nă-chee-bĭ) Young Buck

HOO ~ (Haw) Porcupine

INUNA-INA ~ (īnoona-eena) "Our People" - also spelled Hinonéeino

NEBESIIBEHE ~ (Ney-beh-see-beh-heh) Grandfather

NEINOO ~ (Nay-naw) Mother

NEISONOO ~ (Nay-sah-naw) Father

NONO'EINOC ~ (Nah-nah Ay-nahch) Flatbread

NOYOOT HISEIHIHI ~ (Naw-yawd Hĭ-seh-hĭhĭ) Rainbow Girl

POPO AGIE ~ (Po-po zsha) Crow Indian word for tall (rye) grass river.

SITEE HIITONIH'INOO ~ (Sĭdă hee-dawn-ih-ĭnaw) Fire
Owner

TOUS ~ (toce) greeting among women or from a man to a
woman.

WO'TEENOX ~ (Wah-dă nock) BlackBear

Other books by this author:

Daddy's Boots

But... What If?

Momma's Boots

Grandpa, What If?

What Does a Hero Look Like?

Mixed Up!

Pickysaurus Mac

Hallie of the Harvey Houses

Look for the second installment in the adventure series of Jones, JEEP, Buck & Blue:

**Stuck in the Middle
with Jones, JEEP, Buck & Blue**

Coming soon

Follow the group of misfits' blog:
dailyjjbb.blogspot.com

Contact the author:
www.smlinhart.com

Thanks for reading!

39838103R00246

Made in the USA
Charleston, SC
17 March 2015